If only sh...

In her count... ...covered her
masquerade, he would return her immediately to
her brother for fear of political repercussions. The
sheikh's influence was powerful, and so was her
intended groom's.

Allie knew America was different and far from
Munir. But Cord's neighbors were conducting
business with her brother Rafe; the Coleman
family might urge Cord to send her home even
if he didn't wish to do so himself.

Men, it seemed to her, always stuck together.

Despite Cord's suspicions, she dared not tell
Cord the truth. Not yet. Not until she had no
other choice.

Yet it was her own heart that troubled her the
most. The yearning she had felt as Cord caressed
her palms. Her desperate urge to place her lips on
his.

To experience for the first time a man's kiss...

Dear Reader,

Heartwarming, emotional, compelling...these are all words that describe Harlequin American Romance. Check out this month's stellar selection of love stories, which are sure to please.

First, the BRIDES OF THE DESERT ROSE continuity series continues with *At the Rancher's Bidding* by Charlotte Maclay. In the delightful story, a princess masquerades as her lady-in-waiting to save herself from an arranged marriage—and ends up falling for a rugged rancher.

Also available this month, bestselling author Judy Christenberry's *Randall Honor* resumes her successful BRIDES FOR BROTHERS series about the Randall family of Wyoming. Although they'd shared a night of passion, Victoria Randall wasn't in the market for a husband...and Dr. Jon Wilson had some serious romancing to do if he was going to get this Randall woman to love and honor him!

Next, when an heiress-in-disguise overhears a handsome executive bet his friend that he could win any woman—including her—she's determined to teach him a lesson. Don't miss *Catching the Corporate Playboy* by Michele Dunaway. And rounding out the month is *Stranded at Cupid's Hideaway*, a wonderful reunion romance story from talented author Connie Lane, making her series romance debut.

This month, and every month, come home to Harlequin American Romance—and enjoy!

Best,

Melissa Jeglinski
Associate Senior Editor
Harlequin American Romance

AT THE RANCHER'S BIDDING

Charlotte Maclay

HARLEQUIN®

TORONTO • NEW YORK • LONDON
AMSTERDAM • PARIS • SYDNEY • HAMBURG
STOCKHOLM • ATHENS • TOKYO • MILAN • MADRID
PRAGUE • WARSAW • BUDAPEST • AUCKLAND

Special thanks and acknowledgment are given to
Charlotte Maclay for her contribution to the
BRIDES OF THE DESERT ROSE series.

With special thanks to Mindy and Debbi,
with whom I am linked through both friendship
and the love of writing. You're awesome, ladies!

ISBN 0-373-16929-9

AT THE RANCHER'S BIDDING

Copyright © 2002 by Harlequin Books S.A.

Visit us at www.eHarlequin.com

Printed in U.S.A.

ABOUT THE AUTHOR

Charlotte Maclay can't resist a happy ending. That's why she's had such fun writing more than twenty titles for Harlequin American Romance, Duets and Love & Laughter, plus several Silhouette Romance books, as well. Particularly well-known for her volunteer efforts in her hometown of Torrance, California, Charlotte says her philosophy is that you should make a difference in your community. She and her husband have two married daughters and four grandchildren, whom they are occasionally allowed to baby-sit. She loves to hear from readers and can be reached at P.O. Box 505, Torrance, CA 90508.

Books by Charlotte Maclay

HARLEQUIN AMERICAN ROMANCE

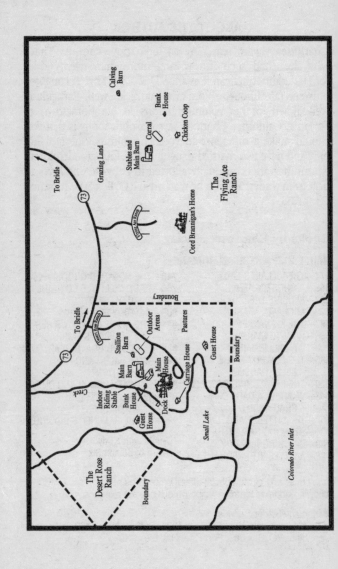

Chapter One

She had one chance to experience freedom and a small taste of independence. She intended to seize that opportunity for as long as she could hold on to it.

The heat of summer pressing down on her, Princess Aliah Bahram hurried across the grounds of the Desert Rose Ranch, following her brother, Sheikh Ashraf. As she ran, the gold bracelets on her arm jingled and her necklaces moved against her throat.

The sheikh was making his daily visit to the Coleman stables to check on the mare pregnant with the foal he had agreed to purchase. Completely enamored by the award-winning Arabians raised here, he had haunted the ranch since their arrival in Bridle, Texas, which was located in the hill country northwest of Austin.

But tomorrow they would return to their own country of Munir, on the Persian Gulf. Aliah—or Allie, as people had begun to call her in America—could not bear the thought of going home. Not when faced with an arranged marriage to a man she could never love,

Sardar Bin Douri. Even the thought sent a shudder of revulsion down her spine.

Her chance to avoid that fate had come yesterday when Leila, her lady-in-waiting, had lost control of her horse while they were riding together. Spooked by blowing dust, the animal had run away with her. A neighboring rancher, Cord Brannigan, had rescued her.

Saved Leila's life!

Sometime during the night, Allie had realized she could take advantage of an ancient Munir custom to gain her liberation—at least temporarily. The possibility inspired her to action now.

"Rafe! Wait for me."

Her brother, looking very distinguished in his white robe, white *gutrah* and black banded *ogal*, slowed near the outdoor riding ring and turned toward her. "What is it, Sister?"

Breathlessly, she came to a halt. "I was wondering if you had made the appropriate arrangements for Leila."

He looked at her blankly. "Is there something wrong with her?"

"No, not at all. I simply assumed you would be honoring our ancient tradition."

"Which tradition is that?"

"You do recall how the Colemans' neighbor—" she hesitated, as though she couldn't think of his name "—Brannigan, I believe he is called, rescued my lady-in-waiting."

"I am sure she was grateful."

"More than grateful, as we should be, too."

Impatiently, he glanced over his shoulder toward the stables, then back to her. "Aliah, I don't know what you are trying to say."

In the name of Constantine, she was going to have to spell it out to her brother! Some days he was terribly dense. Perhaps all brothers were.

"Rafe, the man saved Leila's *life*. In order to properly express our gratitude for saving a servant from sure death, we must present Leila to him as a gift. From this day forward, it is right and just that she *belong* to him."

"You must be joking! That custom went out with—"

"Rafe, you will soon lead our country. There is already talk among our people that you have become too westernized." That wasn't true, or at least she had not heard such a rumor. Nor did she intend for Leila to remain in America with Mr. Brannigan. But Allie couldn't allow her brother to learn her real plan—to stay here herself until either Rafe or the rancher discovered the masquerade she intended. "The gifting of a servant to one who has saved the servant's life is a tradition our people recognize and respect."

"I am not about to leave Leila here against her will." He walked away from Allie.

Doggedly, she followed in his footsteps. "But Leila *wants* to stay. I have already spoken with her." Another lie, but a necessary one at this point.

"Why? Have you been cruel to her?"

"Of course not." Allie huffed in frustration, having

to hurry to keep up with him. "My brother, if you do not support our ancient traditions, our people will respect you less and you will not be able to lead them. Surely there is some way you can follow our customs without offending your own sense of right and wrong."

Without slowing his pace, he slanted her a look. "Why is it I think you have some scheme up your sleeve that would not receive my approval?"

"I have no idea what you mean."

He chuckled, a deep baritone laugh much like their father's, but she could also see he was considering her words.

"All right, as it happens, Cade Coleman mentioned that one of Mr. Brannigan's house servants was away for a few weeks. *If* Leila is agreeable, I will *loan* her to Brannigan for that period of time."

Excitement filled Allie's chest. She'd been given her ticket to freedom. "Leila will be most pleased, I assure you. If you will make the arrangements, I will inform her of the good news."

Without waiting for her brother to change his mind, she raced back toward the main house.

The sprawling hacienda-style house sat on a hill overlooking a lake that flowed into the Colorado River. At night, Allie, Rafe and their party stayed in a small motel in the nearby town of Bridle. During the day, the Colemans had been gracious enough to allow Allie and her servant to use one of the guest rooms upstairs for rest and relaxation.

Allie hurried there now.

"I have wonderful news," she said, bursting into the room.

Leila looked up from her needlework. "I hope that does not mean our departure for Munir will be delayed past tomorrow."

"You will leave on time, I promise." Allie paced to the French doors to look outside, wondering how to phrase her plan to gain Leila's cooperation. At the edge of the veranda a trellis laden with pink-and-white roses stood—her favorite flowers—but today they did little to calm her excitement. "Although I don't know why you are so anxious to return."

"I know I have behaved inappropriately, my mistress. But in the bazaar at home there is a young man...."

Leila's admission had Allie whirling around to look at her servant. She was an attractive woman, slightly younger than her own twenty-two years. She had the same dark eyes that were so common in their country, and she and Allie were of the same height and figure. They both wore simple sheath dresses and sandals, although the fabric of Allie's dress was finer, her sandals a better quality of leather.

"You have a boyfriend?" Allie asked, surprised by a tug of envy. She'd never been allowed in the bazaar unescorted, and certainly never had the opportunity to attract the attention of a young man.

"We have only spoken once." Dipping her head, Leila studied her needlework. "But he does have eyes for me."

"You are a fortunate woman, Leila."

"I will think of myself as fortunate if I get to return to him soon."

Allie knelt beside Leila, taking her needlework from her hands and setting it aside. "You want to go home, and you shall, but I wish to stay in America for a time."

"I doubt your brother will permit—"

"I know. But I have a plan. Because the neighboring rancher saved your life yesterday, the shiekh is going to give you to him as a gift."

Leila paled. "You can't mean—"

"Hear me out. Please. *You* will go home as me, and I will remain here as you."

"What?" Her servant looked at Allie as though she had lost her mind. "My mistress, someone will notice—"

"Nonsense. My brother pays me little attention. And this cowboy saw us only when we were properly covered, as women of Munir should be." Females were expected to wear the cloak and veil in public, and it grated on Allie more than she cared to admit. Her irritation had grown even stronger the longer she remained in America. She envied the freedom women had here, and craved a small taste of that sense of independence.

"But what would happen if the sheikh discovers—"

"Are you not willing to risk whatever punishment my brother might mete out in order to see your friend from the bazaar again?"

Leila hesitated, then responded in a desperate whisper. ''Yes.''

Raising her own fist in victory, Allie began to make plans how they would deceive both her brother and this cowboy, Cord Brannigan. He would be the easiest to fool, she was sure. He had seen neither Leila nor Allie clearly. If she kept her head turned away from her brother, Allie was confident he would not know she had switched places with her servant.

And then, for however long it took her brother to miss her—which might be a few days or even a few weeks—she would be free to explore the world as an ordinary woman. No longer a princess betrothed to a man she could not bear the thought of lying with as a wife.

Later, after her grand adventure, she would be able to deal better with the realities of her life, she told herself.

But for whatever time she was permitted, she would be free!

THE NEXT TIME he saw a runaway horse, he was going to turn his mount in the opposite direction and get out of Dodge in a hurry. From now on damsels in distress would have to manage on their own.

Cord Brannigan drove his pickup out the arching entrance of the Flying Ace Ranch and headed down the dirt road toward the Desert Rose. A plume of dust rose behind the truck, and the cattle grazing in the nearby pasture lazily raised their heads, probably hoping he'd drop off a bale of hay to make life easier for them. *Not this time, ladies.*

He'd tried to tell the visiting sheikh he didn't expect any thanks for rescuing the young woman, and didn't want or need an extra servant. For the past year, he'd lived alone in the ranch house with his half sister, Brianna. Even though his housekeeper was gone for a few weeks, helping with a new grandchild, Cord and Brianna could get along fine without help. And his hired hands pretty much took care of themselves.

But Sheikh Rafe didn't know the meaning of "no, thanks." It had become obvious that if Cord pressed the issue he was likely to cause an international incident. At the very least, he'd cause trouble between the sheikh and the Coleman family, who were trying to sell the guy a foal from one of their prize mares.

Cord didn't want to cause a problem for his neighbors. The Colemans—particularly Alex, Cade and Mac—had been friends of his for years. The three brothers were sheikhs in their own right. But since they had been raised in Texas, Cord didn't feel a need to kowtow to them. Causing them to lose a customer was a different matter.

So Cord was stuck with a servant he didn't need. Unless he could talk the woman into going somewhere else.

Pulling up in front of the two-story Desert Rose ranch house, he parked the truck. The horse pastures were greener here than on his ranch, the grass richer for the pampered Arabians, the fences white-painted wood rather than barbed wire. He preferred the more rugged work of raising cattle, but the Colemans had certainly made an international name for themselves in the horse business.

He got out of the truck and nodded a greeting as Cade Coleman came out of the house. "How's the new daddy bearing up?" Cord asked.

"Better than Rena," he said with a smile that made his dark eyes light up. "She's got to handle most of the nighttime duties with the twins. But neither one of us has gotten much sleep in the past three months."

"I can imagine." The front door opened, and Cord looked up to see the sheikh in his flowing white garb, followed by a woman fully cloaked and veiled, with only her dark, almond-shaped eyes visible. "Are you sure there isn't some way I can refuse Sheikh Rafe's gift?" he asked Cord under his breath.

Cade lifted his shoulders in an easy shrug of indifference. "It's a custom, I guess. You'll think of some way to handle it."

Cord wasn't so sure.

"Good afternoon." Rafe extended his hand, griping Cord's firmly. "Allow me to present Leila, my sister's lady-in-waiting. She is honored to be chosen to serve for a short time the man who saved her life."

"Look, Rafe, this really isn't necessary. I only did what any man would do." He hadn't been particularly heroic. Had just been at the right place at the right time, or rather the wrong place, as it turned out.

The sheikh waved off his objection and instead beckoned the woman to step forward. She carried a small satchel with her. All her worldly possessions, Cord imagined.

Cord tipped the brim of his Stetson. "Miss." Actually, he didn't have a clue if she was a miss or a missus, there being no way to judge her age under all those yards of cotton fabric. With her head bowed, he couldn't even see her eyes, although he remembered them as dark orbs circled with kohl, looking very frightened when he'd reined in her horse.

When he took the satchel from her, he did catch a glimpse of her hands. Long, delicate fingers and soft, unblemished skin the shade of cream right from a mother cow... Not exactly the hands of someone used to hard work, although there were no rings or any sign of extravagant wealth.

"If she does not please you," Rafe said, "return her to me, and I shall make amends."

Studying the shiekh's solemn expression, Cord wondered if there was the hint of a threat there—that Leila would suffer if she didn't live up to expectations. "I'm sure she'll be fine." Hell, this wasn't like buying a broodmare with a guaranteed money-back deal that she'd produce for him.

"The sheikh and his sister are returning to Munir early tomorrow," Cade said.

"I have business to attend to and Aliah—Allie, as my sister is called here—must prepare for her wedding to Sardar Bin Douri, a man of wealth and influence in my country. The event is much anticipated by our people. There will be great rejoicing when the two families are joined."

"Well then, have yourself a good trip, Rafe. Come back and visit anytime," Cord said.

"No doubt I shall. The Coleman stables at the Desert Rose offer many enticements."

Cord chuckled. From what he'd heard, the sheikh's stables were something to brag about, too.

He said his goodbyes and carried the bag to his truck, tossing it in the back. Silently, Leila walked a steady three paces behind him, which raised the hackles on his neck. This whole deal was crazy!

She waited for him to open the door. He took her elbow, helping her up, and felt the fragility of her bones through her dress. Munir didn't raise their women very sturdy, he mused. Not like Texas women, who could ride a horse and rope cows all day, then party all night and make love until dawn.

And be unfaithful in the process, playing a man for a fool, as he had learned the hard way.

As they reached the road leaving the Desert Rose, and still Leila hadn't spoken word one, Cord pulled the truck to the side and stopped.

"Look, Leila, you're probably not any happier about this arrangement than I am."

"I am not unhappy." With fingers that trembled slightly, she lowered her veil. Beautiful was an understatement. Her kohl-ringed eyes stood out above dramatically sculpted cheekbones. Her unpainted lips were a natural rose and they glistened when she licked them before smiling at him. "I am most happy to be your servant as long as I shall please you."

Cord swallowed hard as the rest of his body took

particular note of the young woman's features. Nope, this kind of gift wasn't one a man could accept.

"Do you have any family or friends in the States? I could take you to the Austin airport. It's not that far away. I'll get you a ticket on any airline you want, to any place you'd like to go." Including all the way back to Munir, if that's what she wanted.

Her dark eyes flickered. "No, I have no family here. No friends. This is my first visit to your country."

"Then you could get a job somewhere. Start a new life. Or just plain take a vacation till it's time to go home."

"No, I do not think that would be possible." Allie clasped her hands together, knowing she did not have the skills—or the courage—to run that far from her responsibilities. She had no money. No green card that would allow her to work, assuming she was capable of being anything other than a princess. How would she survive on her own? "I wish to go to your ranch and work in your household." A rich man would have many servants, and in a large household she could conceal both her identity and her lack of training as a servant.

He leaned his head back and sighed. Despite his apparent distress, his appearance was quite appealing, if more rugged than the few men she had known in her own country. The angle of his jaw was a little sharper and stronger, and a slight bump on his nose suggested it had once been broken. There was a tiny scar below his right eyebrow.

But his eyes fascinated Allie the most—not dark brown like those of her countrymen, but a lighter shade, filled with the greens and golds of this verdant countryside. She would like to make a study of them. Each time she looked into his eyes, they changed color with the sun or shade and became all the more intriguing.

"Okay, Leila, I'll make you a deal. I'll hire you as my housekeeper for now and pay you a decent wage. You can save your money until you can go out on your own. Or if you get fed up with ranch life, I'll put you on a plane back home and explain to Rafe. If he gives you a hard time he'll have to answer to me."

Her eyes widened with pleasure. "How much will you pay me?"

He blinked at her question, then named a price that astounded her.

"I accept your offer, Mr. Brannigan."

Shaking his head, he said, "Cord will do. We're not exactly formal in these parts."

"That is fine by me, as you Americans say. I have had enough formality to last me a lifetime."

As he shifted the truck into gear, pulling back onto the road, Allie smiled to herself. To think she'd have a paying job *and* the freedom of an American woman. What amazing good fortune—for however long she was allowed to enjoy it.

BACK AT THE DESERT ROSE, Cade had watched Cord's truck drive away, and followed the path of the dust cloud as it swept down the road behind it. Something was odd, he mused.

While he'd visited Balahar, his beloved wife's homeland in the Middle East, he'd had a chance to observe the behavior of a good many servants. The kingdom employed hundreds of cooks and maids, valets and assorted other workers who were almost invisible, they were so subservient.

The woman who had left with Cord was... different.

Though she'd kept her face averted, her head hadn't been bowed as deeply as most servants he'd seen. Her back had been a little too straight, her stride a little too confident. It had made him think that Leila wasn't a servant at all but rather—

But no, that wasn't possible.

No pampered princess of Munir or any other member of Middle Eastern royalty would run off to be a housekeeper at a cattle ranch. The thought of Princess Allie scrubbing floors was laughable.

He frowned a little, realizing his own wife, a princess of Balahar, had taken to domestic chores with far more enthusiasm than he'd had any right to expect. And she wore motherhood like a golden crown.

Behind him, Rafe cleared his throat. "I thought I would visit the paddocks to see how Khalahari is faring this afternoon. Would you care to join me?"

"Sure." Tucking his fingertips in the pockets of his jeans, Cade walked beside Rafe. The sheikh was as fanatic about his Arabians as Cade was. Rafe couldn't wait for Khalahari, the prize mare of the

Desert Rose, to foal. If Cade would let him, Rafe would probably take the mare back to Munir with him.

Cade could understand that. He'd been obsessed with the ranch and his Arabians until he'd had a family of his own. Marriage had been the first step. But when Rena gave birth to the twins—Zach and Natalie—Cade discovered nothing in the world could compare to being a husband and father.

WHEN IT SEEMED as though they had been driving for a long while along a dirt track, Allie grew anxious. She had thought Cord a neighbor of the Colemans' Desert Rose Ranch. So far she had seen nothing but grass wilted by the summer heat, elms and oaks spaced by nature to provide splashes of shade, and cows lazily chewing their cuds.

"How much farther to your cattle ranch?" she asked.

"We've been on Flying Ace land for about five minutes now, but the house is a ways yet."

"Your ranch is that big?"

"Big enough. A couple of thousand acres."

"But that is larger than the Desert Rose."

"Yep. Cows need more land than horses. You gotta keep moving them around, changing pastures so they don't overeat the grass."

He must be a wealthy man, indeed, Allie thought. "This name, Flying Ace—where did it come from?"

He shot her a grin that creased his cheek and made

him look far younger and even more attractive than only a moment ago.

"Rumor has it my grandfather won the ranch in a poker game."

"An ace flew from the deck into his hand, yes?"

"More likely it flew out of his sleeve into his hand."

She stared at him blankly, then choked on a laugh when she realized what he meant. "Your grandfather *cheated?*"

"Now, he never 'fessed up to such a thing. But word has it no cowboy for a hundred miles around ever sat down at a poker table with him again."

She did laugh then, delighted with the prospect of living on Cord Brannigan's ranch for some amount of time. At the palace her brother was so dour, so serious, she rarely saw him laugh. Only in the women's quarters could she relax and be herself. Even then she had to use caution not to make an error in protocol. Or be too friendly with her ladies-in-waiting. Heaven forbid she should make a scene at the local bazaar or spend too much money on fripperies like scarves and shoes. Word would get back to her brother.

He was so confoundedly *bossy!* At least with her that was true.

She could only sympathize with a woman who found herself married to Rafe, subject to his arrogance and unbending ways.

Though the air was warm blowing in the open truck windows, she shivered with distaste at the thought of marriage and her betrothed. She vowed to view each moment of freedom at the Flying Ace as a taste of ambrosia. She would fill herself with memories to last a lifetime.

Only then would she be able to face the future she dreaded.

Chapter Two

Allie's breath caught at her first glimpse of the Flying Ace ranch house. Although not as large as the one at the Desert Rose, the sprawling adobe structure seemed to fit into the landscape as if nature had put it there. A wrought-iron gate stood open to welcome visitors, and Cord drove the truck beneath an arched entry into an inner courtyard. It was almost like entering the palace grounds in Munir, but without the guards at the gate.

America was indeed a wonderful country. So free and open. A safe haven—albeit a temporary one for her.

"Your home is lovely," she said as he parked beside a stone walkway leading to a covered entry and a wide wooden door.

"We make do." His modest response made her smile.

Excitement fluttered through her midsection as he escorted her up the walkway, his hand pressing lightly at the small of her back. Had she expected a butler to greet them at the door, she would have been disappointed. Instead, Cord simply lifted the latch, shoved open the door and ushered her inside.

The temperature was ten degrees cooler in the dim interior of the high-ceiling great room than it was outside, the recessed windows in the wide adobe walls preventing direct sunlight from penetrating. Heavy oak furniture and comfortable leather couches were arranged around a large fireplace that no doubt heated the room efficiently in winter. Paintings of horses and Western landscapes decorated the walls.

He dropped her bag on one of the couches. "Brianna!" he shouted.

"In here," a woman's voice answered.

"Come meet our new, uh, housekeeper."

Troubled, Allie frowned. She had not thought to ask of Cord's marital status or if he had a concubine living with him. But perhaps Brianna was simply one of his servants.

A pretty woman with a long blond ponytail appeared from down the hallway. Fresh faced and no older than Allie, she wore jeans and a cotton blouse tucked in at the waist.

"Leila, I'd like you to meet my sister, Brianna Taylor. She handles the ranch's bookkeeping and keeps the paperwork flowing for me."

"Hi," the young woman said, smiling. "I didn't really think the sheikh would, you know—"

"Sheikh Ashraf does very much as he pleases,"

Allie said, wishing she didn't have to defend her brother.

"I, uh, made a deal with Leila to put her on the payroll as a housekeeper while she's here," Cord interjected.

Looking puzzled, Brianna nodded. "Fine. I'll put together the paperwork."

He cleared his throat. "I thought maybe you'd show Leila to Maria's room, get her settled there, at least temporarily."

"Maria?" Allie questioned.

"Our housekeeper," Brianna explained. "She's visiting her daughter in El Paso to help with a new baby."

"Oh, but you do have other servants, yes?"

"Five or six hired hands, depending on the time of year," Cord said. "They stay in the bunkhouse out back, but I sure wouldn't want them to hear you calling 'em servants."

"There is no one else?"

"Nope. With just me and Brianna, we don't need a whole lot of help around the house."

Panic twisted in Allie's belly. How could such a big ranch have only one servant? She would not be able to hide. Too soon they would know the truth.

Picking up her satchel, Cord tried to pass it to his sister.

Brianna stepped back a pace, her gaze dancing between her brother and Allie, a curious smile playing across her face. "Look, I was right in the middle of doing the quarterly reports. Why don't you show Leila to her room, give her a tour of the place?''

Allie leaped at the possibility. Surely a woman would more quickly discover her masquerade than a man. She would be better off with Cord as her guide. "Yes, a tour would be nice. Thank you." She smiled her warmest smile.

Hesitating, Cord looked as if he was about to refuse, his eyes roving over Allie in a probing way that started her heart beating faster. Then he nodded curtly. "Okay. Your room is this way."

Without giving his sister another glance, Allie followed Cord through a spacious dining room in the opposite direction from which Brianna had earlier appeared. The more distance she kept from the other woman, the better.

In the large kitchen, there was another table, though not as big as the one in the dining room. Stainless-steel appliances looked new and efficient. At least she supposed they were efficient. Allie had little idea how any of them operated. The kitchens were not a part of the palace she visited often, not since she'd sneaked in there as a child.

Immediately adjacent to the kitchen, Cord stopped at a doorway. "Okay, here's your room."

She stood at the threshold while he stepped inside. A handmade quilt covered the modest-size bed, doilies edged with crocheting protected the top of a walnut chest of drawers, and a small, colorful hooked rug lay beside the bed on the wooden floor. Quaint. And smaller than her dressing room at the palace.

"You've got your own bathroom and TV," Cord said.

Swallowing her dismay at the simple quarters, she said, "I am sure I will be quite comfortable." Gaining her freedom, however briefly, had its price.

"You can get settled in and—"

"I would very much like to see the rest of the ranch, if I may." Feeling the cloak she wore was no longer necessary, she unfastened the plain, gray garment and tossed it on the bed, revealing the simple sheath dress she wore. The gold bracelets and necklaces she normally wore she had sent home with Leila. "I have never before visited a cattle ranch."

Cord's eyes widened. Damned if they didn't nearly fall out of their sockets, he thought. He stuffed his hands in his jeans pockets, trying to look anywhere except at Leila. Without her billowing cloak, she was more slender than he had imagined, but every inch a woman. The swell of her small breasts pressed against her bodice; her bare arms were as graceful as a dancer's, with tiny wrists a man could span with his finger and thumb. Long, straight hair the color of Texas pecans streamed down her back.

Desperately, he tried to think of some reason to send her back to her home in Munir right away. Or at the very least come up with an excuse why he couldn't give her a tour of the ranch.

He failed on both counts.

"Sure. I'll show you around a little. Then you'll probably want to get dinner started."

"Me?"

"Yeah, that's kind of what housekeepers do. Cook dinner. Clean house. You know."

"But I don't know how to cook."

His brows tugged together as he struggled with indecision. This was not what he had expected. In fact, nothing about Leila was quite what he had expected, including her soft accent with traces of British school English. "Tell me just what is it you did for your, uh, princess." Lord, he hadn't stammered this much since he'd invited Marijane Morgan to the eighth grade dance and then gotten her braces locked with his when he tried to kiss her.

Allie thought fast, trying to recall what it was that Leila did so competently for her, serving her in their women's quarters.

"I prepared my mistress's bath daily, oiled her body, helped her to dress in the finest silk gowns that money can buy. I brushed her hair." Feeling slightly wicked and more adventuresome than she had thought possible, she stepped forward and ran her fingers through the thick waves of Cord's saddle-brown hair. "I could do all of that for you, if you wish."

"No. That's okay." His ruddy complexion flushed even darker and he edged away from her. "Let's, uh, take that tour and we'll deal with the rest of your, uh, responsibilities later."

Shifting her hair in front of her shoulder, she

smiled. She had no wish to argue with his decision. The longer she could put off the reality of being a housekeeper, the happier she would be. Cord, too, if he knew how few domestic skills she possessed.

CORD WAS PROUD of the Flying Ace. Since his father's death five years ago he'd upgraded the facilities and added to the herd through careful breeding and management. It was his home, his life. He poured all of his energy into the ranch and it never disappointed him, even in bad times.

Which was more than he could say about the women in his life.

When Cord had been twelve, his mother had deserted the family. A year ago he'd discovered that she'd gone off because of his father's infidelity—an infidelity that had resulted in Brianna's birth. The unexpected news that he had a half sister had surprised him, but didn't excuse the fact that his mother had abandoned Cord.

A few years ago, he had decided he was ready to settle down, start a family of his own. He had the rings in his pocket when he flew to Houston, where Sandra Maddox, the woman he'd been dating, was working. Problem was, she'd gone off to California the day before with a married man. Cord had been played for a besotted fool.

Nope, these days it didn't pay to trust a woman.

Or perhaps *he* was the problem. He wasn't lovable—either in the eyes of his mother or the woman he'd finally chosen to marry.

He slanted Leila a glance as they walked toward the weathered wood barn and adjoining stables. He couldn't deny that she got his juices going, but she sure wasn't suitable for ranch life. He'd give her a week, two at the most, and she'd be long gone, very likely back to her home country. He loved Texas as much as the next man, but it wasn't an easy place to live, not on a ranch, anyway. The summer could be hotter than Hades, the winters cold enough to freeze the teats off a heifer. In between there was plenty of hard, demanding work, wide-open spaces and a sense of accomplishment he'd never be able to find with a desk job.

"Do they raise any cattle where you come from?" he asked.

Her hair shifted like a veil as she turned toward him, the sun catching the strands and making them gleam like polished agate. "Oh, no, we raise oil. A great deal of it. And we export large quantities of steel and cement. Munir is a very wealthy country."

"Then you like it there?" he asked hopefully. Maybe she'd get homesick and want to go back sooner rather than later.

Her slender shoulders lifted in a shrug of denial. "Women do not have as much freedom there as they do in America."

Reaching the corral, he placed a booted foot on the lower fence rung and leaned his elbow on the top.

"Guess you don't get to ride much at home then, and that's why your mount got away from you."

She lifted her head in a haughty manner and her eyes sparked. "That is not true. I am an excellent—" She stumbled momentarily, obviously remembering the incident. "The horse spooked. Dirt blew in his face. I do not know why he did not respond to my command."

He smiled at her bravado. Two days ago she'd been terrified. Now she was—arrogant.

One of the cow ponies, a dun-colored mare with a darker brown mane, trotted over to the fence and stuck her head over the top. Without hesitation, Leila rubbed the mare's nose and scratched behind her ears.

"Her name is Betsy. You like horses?" he asked.

"Oh, yes. Although this one is not as elegant as my broth—the pure-blooded Arabians in Sheikh Ashraf's stables. Still, she is very pretty."

"She can run rings around any Arabian you can name when it comes to rounding up cattle. Those Arabians are all show and no go, as far as I'm concerned."

She sniffed. "If you say so."

Her comment amused rather than irritated him. "If you stick around long enough, I'll give you a shot at riding one of my cutting horses."

Her interest perked up immediately. "You would do that?"

"Sure. We'll pick you a gentle one. Wouldn't want to risk another runaway."

"I promise, if your horse has been properly trained, I will keep him under control this time."

Despite her previous lapse, Cord pretty much believed Leila. Attitude had a lot to do with a rider's ability to handle a horse. Leila was so self-assured that most of his remuda wouldn't try any shenanigans while she had a hold of the reins. Which made him wonder what had gone wrong earlier in the week.

"Come on. There's more to see." He gestured toward the adjacent barn.

She gave the horse a final rub between the ears, crooning, "I will come again, pretty Betsy, and bring you a carrot next time. Would you like that?" The cow pony nodded her approval.

Cord walked Leila into the barn, standing back to watch her reaction. He could all but see her delicate little nostrils quiver at the earthy scents of hay and manure, leather, neat's-foot oil and liniment.

She turned, a bemused expression on her face. "I was rarely allowed in the stables at the palace. This smells so...alive."

"Yeah." So was she. Caught in a column of sunlight beaming in through the hayloft window, she looked radiant. Glowing with vitality and filled with sensual promise. It was enough to make a man rethink his long stint of celibacy. Which, in this case, was not a good idea. An honorable man did not mess with a woman who was so obviously innocent. At least in this part of Texas, that wasn't done.

A mewling sound came from the back of a nearby stall.

Leila peered in that direction. "Oh, look, a kitten." She slipped into the stall, picking up a young brown-and-black ball of fluff with white paws that looked to be only a few weeks old. "She is so tiny. Where is her mother?"

Cord shrugged with indifference. "Hard to tell. We usually have a couple of barn cats around to take care of the rodents."

"But she should not leave her baby all alone." She rubbed her cheek across the kitten's head. "This little one is lonely and frightened. Hungry, too, I think. Perhaps the mother is injured."

Her concern for a feral cat raised to fend for itself amused Cord. "I'm sure her mom will come back. Why don't you leave the kitten there, and we'll check later."

With obvious reluctance, Leila made a nest of hay in the corner of the stall, murmured reassuring words to the kitten, then tucked her into the nest as though she were putting a baby to bed for the night.

"I will come back later to be sure you are all right, little one. I promise."

He gestured for her to leave the kitten. There were more outbuildings to be seen.

One of his hired hands, Joe Piedmont, picked that moment to come strolling into the barn, his long legs so bowed he could probably walk right over a five-hundred-gallon propane tank without touching the sides.

"Hey, boss," he drawled.

Cord dragged his attention away from Leila. "Joe, this is Leila. She's going to be our housekeeper for a while."

The cowboy's jaw dropped, then he scrambled to yank his battered hat from his head. "Howdy, miss. Glad to meetcha."

She honored him with a dazzling smile. "It is my pleasure, Mr. Joe."

The cowboy's face flamed a bright red, and his Adam's apple bobbed in his scrawny neck.

Cord grimaced. "There somethin' you want from me, Joe?"

"Huh? Oh, yeah." Meeting Leila had obviously caused him to lose his train of thought. In a few more minutes, he'd probably forget his own name. "We was wondering when you wanted us to start weaning the calves."

"Tomorrow would be as good a time as any, assuming the weather holds."

"Gotcha, boss." Struggling to get his hat on straight, he backed toward the wide-open barn door. "Sure was nice to meetcha, miss. The fellas will be real happy to have you around."

"Thank you, Mr. Joe," she said sweetly.

"Joe'll do, miss."

She nodded just as Joe backed into the side of the door, practically knocking himself out. He spun around and hurried outside, moving faster than Cord had seen him go since one of the breeding bulls got stung on the rump by a bee.

Cord stifled a laugh. Getting any work done around the ranch was going to be tough until his hands got used to Leila being there. Which might take quite awhile.

His assessment of the situation was confirmed when Red Galliger happened to amble by while Cord was showing the calving barn to Leila. Ty Thomas and Pablo Ramirez came around to get an eyeful as they passed by the bunkhouse. At the chicken coop, Lester Smith joined the crowd. By the end of the week, Cord figured he'd have cowpokes from every ranch within a fifty-mile radius hanging around.

He wasn't quite sure why that bothered him so much.

Even the old rooster who guarded the henhouse let out an ear-piercing crow of welcome and flapped his wings to show off.

Leila's eyes sparkled with all the attention. "So you raise chickens as well as cows?"

"All the eggs and drumsticks you could ask for," Cord said. "Speaking of which, maybe we ought to let you get started on supper and let my men get back to work." He gave his cowhands a pointed look, which eventually got them moving back to whatever chores Leila's arrival had interrupted.

"As you wish." Leila tossed her head in much the same way the lead mare of a wild herd would, letting the world know that no stallion, however powerful and ambitious, could get her to do a thing she didn't want to.

Cord decided that didn't bode well for him or the Flying Ace Ranch.

ALLIE HAD PROCRASTINATED about as long as she could.

She'd hung her few garments in the minuscule closet, set out her soaps and lotions in the bathroom, which seemed even smaller. Fortunately, when she tested the bed, it appeared to have a firm mattress. She would sleep well. Assuming Cord did not send her packing when he discovered she'd never cooked a meal in her life.

Straightening her shoulders, she walked from her room to the kitchen, which was rather like entering a foreign land. There were so many cupboards, so many gleaming appliances, she didn't know where to begin. Tentatively, she opened the cabinet beneath the sink and frowned at the plastic container half-full of garbage.

"Maria keeps most of the cleaning supplies on the service porch, if that's what you're looking for."

Allie jumped at the sound of Brianna's voice.

"No, I was just getting acquainted with where things are."

"Before Maria left, she stocked the pantry and freezer with enough food to last us a month. I'm sure you'll find everything you need."

Assuming she could *find* the pantry. Leila smiled weakly. "Of course."

"If you've got a minute, I need for you to fill out these papers for my payroll records." She placed a form on the kitchen table along with a ballpoint pen. "You know how the government is about details."

Happy to delay her cooking task, she sat at the table and bent over the form. "Leila Khautori," she printed. For the address she wrote "Flying Ace." She had no idea what the phone number might be, and she certainly had no references or prior employment experience. Finally she slid the form back to Brianna, who looked it over.

"Your social security number?" she asked.

"I do not know what that is."

"You mean you don't know your number, or you don't have one?"

"I am sure I do not have one."

Brianna's smooth forehead puckered into a disapproving frown. "You've really got to have one or I can't handle the taxes and withholding." She thought a moment, visibly trying to think through the problem. "I guess the best thing is for you to apply for one at the Bridle post office, and we can wait till your number arrives to send in the paperwork."

"That would be the same place I can get a green card?"

Wincing, Brianna shook her head and picked up the form Allie had just completed by forging Leila's signature. "Why don't I talk with Cord? I'm sure he has something in mind."

Allie hoped so. "Tell me, Brianna, what kind of food does Cord like to eat?" Something simple, she prayed. Although given Allie's culinary expertise, a bunch of grapes would be the only meal within her capabilities.

"He's not real fussy. Like most bachelors, I suppose. Anything you'd like to fix I'm sure would be fine with him. He does like his coffee black and strong, though, particularly in the morning."

Given the proper ingredients, that was one thing Allie felt she could handle. "And this pantry you speak of?"

Brianna's gaze slid to a door next to the entrance to Allie's bedroom. "That's it. What you don't find there will probably be in the fridge or in one of these cupboards. There's also a freezer in the barn with a side of beef in it, but you probably won't need that."

Not likely. "You have been most helpful. Thank you."

"Don't plan anything fancy. We usually eat here in the kitchen when it's just the two of us."

"Eating with the servants. How democratic."

Brianna gave her an odd look, nodded, then left the kitchen, shaking her head.

Allie exhaled the breath she'd been holding. Dinner was likely to be an interesting experience for all concerned.

In the pantry, Allie found shelves of canned

goods—fruits, vegetables, soups and something called chili con carne—plus tins of flour and sugar. Surely somewhere within this bounty Allie could find something to warm for supper, *if* she could figure out how to operate the stove. To her relief, she also found a bin of fresh peaches and apricots, a few oranges and some apples.

A hurried visit to the double-door refrigerator produced several varieties of cheese. Crackers appeared as if by magic in one of the over-the-counter cupboards. The makings of a true feast.

Feeling more confident by the minute, she scurried around, locating silverware and plates, which she set on the table. No evening meal was complete without candles, which she found in a drawer. The simple white color and their stubby shape did not please her, but it was the best she could find.

Her search for wine failed to produce any, but perhaps Cord preferred coffee with his evening meal, as well as in the morning. The brand of coffee she found was unfamiliar to her, but remembering the local brew had seemed weak at the Desert Rose, she doubled the grounds. Fortunately, the women's quarters at the palace had adopted the use of an electric coffeemaker, so she was familiar with that appliance.

Finally, drawing a deep breath, she was ready to announce dinner.

CORD HAD SHOWERED and his hair was still wet as he walked into the kitchen. He glanced at the table with its three place settings and the emergency candles sticking up from a grouping of coffee cups as though from a newfangled candelabra. Bowls of fruit and plates of cheese and crackers provided an interesting centerpiece. Sniffing the air, all he could detect was the rich aroma of coffee, and he wondered what the main course could be.

With a flourish, Leila gestured toward his place at the head of the table. She looked flushed, the hair at her temple dark with perspiration. "I hope you enjoy your meal."

"I'm looking forward to it." He pulled out his chair and sat down. "Besides the fruit and appetizers, what's the main course?"

Brianna, looking fresh and well scrubbed, took her place at the opposite end of the table. She was wearing one of her inscrutable smiles, suggesting she knew something he didn't.

"My master," Leila said solemnly, seating herself between them. "Your sister assured me whatever I might prepare would please you. And in such hot weather, I know my appetite wanes. I'm sure yours does as well."

He surveyed the table one more time. "This is it?"

"A meal fit for a sheikh, I assure you."

Cord sputtered, not wanting to criticize too harshly. But he was a meat-and-potatoes man in all of the related variations. Fruit and cheese just didn't cut it.

"You haven't even peeled the oranges," he muttered as his stomach growled. "How do you expect—"

"As you wish, master." With a flick of her wrist, Allie picked up an orange and used her table knife to slice through the skin. She sectioned it, then separated the halves.

Juice squirted in a fountain as she divided the sections one by one. The air filled with the scent of citrus, conjuring images of a desert kingdom where thirst was quenched with fruit. She licked her thumb and forefinger, savoring the taste with deliberation, her tongue circling each finger in turn. All the while her dark, exotic eyes focused on Cord.

She pulled the next segment apart and Cord began to sweat.

There was something incredibly sexy about the juice running down her fingers, circling her wrist, and the way she tongued it off. Leisurely. As though she was anxious to enjoy every last drop.

Any man with a modicum of good sense would know he shouldn't be so fascinated. Know the press against the fly of his jeans was pure, unadulterated lust. Know he had to get the hell out of here.

He shoved back his chair from the table. "Seems to me there was some leftover roast beef in the refrigerator. I think I'll make myself a sandwich, if nobody minds."

Brianna ducked her head and turned away, but not, Cord suspected, because she was feeling shy. Her tittering laughter made him glad he hadn't had a sister while he'd been fighting the changes in his body and lack of control during adolescence. Which seemed to be the syndrome he was experiencing now, despite being nearly thirty-five years old.

"Brianna tells me I must have a social security number," Leila says, "and that I should apply at the postal authority in Bridle."

He glanced over his shoulder to see her placing the sectioned fruit on his plate. "Yeah?"

"You will take me there tomorrow, and I will also purchase new clothes. What I have brought with me is totally inadequate for my new housekeeper responsibilities."

Cord had trouble disagreeing with that. If he'd had his way, she'd be wearing her voluminous cloak. He could only hope in Bridle she'd buy an equally concealing outfit. A burlap sack sounded about right to him.

Even so, it grated that she was ordering *him* around. Just who did she think she was? A princess?

Chapter Three

After dinner—such as it was—Cord went into the ranch office with Brianna to check on the quarterly reports she'd finished. He sat down behind the big oak desk that used to be his father's and tipped back in the swivel chair, making the springs creak. He picked up the forms.

"How'd we do this quarter?"

"After culling the herd, the cash flow looks good. I'd say there's no reason you can't reinvest some of the funds in new breeding stock." In the past year, since she'd moved to the Flying Ace, Brianna had begun to show more confidence in her predictions.

"Good. Glad to hear that." He flipped through the pages, grateful for her help. Paperwork had always been a drudgery for Cord. "I'll probably take a trip into Austin early next week for the stock sale."

"Would you like me to print out the catalog of offerings? It's on the Internet."

"Thanks. I'd appreciate that." He handed her back the report and watched as she took her seat at her desk across the room from his. "So what do you think of our new housekeeper?"

"I think if she's been doing the cooking back in Munir, the sheikh was less than generous to make you a gift of her."

Cord muttered his agreement, feeling a smile tug at his lips.

"You'll need to be patient with her," Brianna warned. "She doesn't appear to be a very experienced housekeeper."

"Yeah, I know. But I doubt she'll want to hang around long."

Brianna shot him a quick smile, then turned to her computer. "I don't know, big brother. She may surprise you. And you'll have to give her points for dinner. She certainly had your attention."

Cord wasn't ready to admit anything of the sort, sure as hell not to his little sister.

"I also think if you want to pay her, we'll have to pay her under the table."

"How's that?"

Brianna glanced over her shoulder. "No green card, Cord. My guess is her visa is temporary and doesn't allow for employment."

"We'll work out something." Frowning thoughtfully, he picked up a copy of the *Cattlemen* magazine from his desk and thumbed through the pages. But his heart wasn't in the nutrient levels of various grasslands around the country. Instead he kept wondering what Leila was up to.

The catalog Brianna printed out before she went to

her room didn't hold his interest, either, and it should have. Picking the right bull at the right price with all the right attributes was what made his breeding program a success.

But at the moment he couldn't seem to concentrate on the expected progeny differences of the bulls that would be on sale.

Yawning, he finally decided to call it quits for the night. He'd check the catalog tomorrow or the next day when he was more alert—and not so distracted by thoughts of his new housekeeper.

The lights were still on in the kitchen. When he went to switch them off, he noticed a movement outside in the halo of the barn light. Frowning, he wondered who or what would be out and about at this hour. Ranchers hit the sack early. He and his ranch hands were no exception.

He stepped outside and let his eyes adjust to the darkness. The air had cooled considerably from the daytime high in the nineties, but it still held the moisture so common during the summer months in Texas. The call of crickets filled the air along with the soft sound of horses and cattle settling down for the night. Not a breath of wind stirred.

There was a stream of something else in the still air, however, not just the animal smells he'd grown up with on the ranch. A tropical scent like jasmine. He followed it toward the barn.

The door moaned in protest as he opened it. Across the way, he saw the shadow of a slender woman slip into a vacant horse stall. He should have known she'd be back to check on the cat.

"Couldn't leave it alone, could you?"

She screamed. Whatever she'd been carrying flew up in the air and conked him on the forehead. Cool liquid ran down his face, and he licked his lips. *Milk.*

"Easy, princess, it's me. Cord."

"I am *not* a princess. I am your housekeeper. And you nearly scared the life out of me. What in the name of Constantine are you doing following me?"

"Trying to figure out who's sneaking around my barn."

"Well!" she huffed. "You frightened Mittens, too. And now I don't have any milk for her."

"Mittens?"

"The kitten. Her little paws are pure white. It is a good name."

It was, assuming you wanted to name the offspring of a feral cat that came and went as it pleased. "Its mother—"

"Has not returned." In the shadows, Leila bent, picking up a handful of fur. "I am going to feed Mittens, unless you refuse to allow me the privilege."

"Be my guest." He could only hope the immigration rules in Munir allowed for the admission of cats from the States without months of quarantine when Leila returned home.

"Thank you. You are most kind."

Imperiously, with the kitten cuddled against her chest, she swept past him, and he grinned. Suddenly he wondered if Brianna was right. Sheikh Rafe might have been well rid of his household servant, the runaway horse rescue only an excuse to ship her off to someone else for a few weeks.

Unexpected sympathy tugged at his conscience. Here was a young woman who'd been virtually torn from her homeland, landing in a situation totally foreign to her, and her biggest concern was for a six-week-old kitten abandoned by its mother. Perhaps there was more depth to Leila than he had imagined.

That arrogant tilt of her head that was so intriguing—and equally annoying—could well be her way to disguise her fears.

ALLIE SLIPPED BETWEEN the sheets in her bedroom, but she suspected sleep would elude her for some hours, and it would not be entirely the fault of the kitten, who was so fascinated by her toes, pouncing on them.

Through the open window she heard the night sounds of the ranch. A horse moving in its stall. Crickets chirping. And in the distance, the occasional lowing of a cow. Pleasant, restful sounds, if only she could relax.

She had thought no one had seen her enter the barn, and Cord had nearly frightened her to death. He was so tall, as much a giant as the guards who protected the palace in Munir, and so broad shouldered, he'd given her quite a start. But his voice, a rich baritone, had a far different effect on her than any palace guard. One she hadn't previously experienced. Her heart had taken off like a drummer in the palace marching band.

Her breath had grown as shallow as an aging woman about to faint in the heat of midday.

Allie sighed and tried to snare Mittens, who was determined to burrow under the sheet and find her way to Allie's bare feet, where her tiny teeth could gnaw at will. A few laps of milk in the kitchen had turned the kitten into a frisky pest.

"Behave yourself, Mittens," she admonished, not quite able to keep the smile from her voice.

Whatever was she going to do about Cord? She had so little experience with men that she had no idea how she should act around him. Particularly since she was supposed to be his servant. Humph! If the truth were known, she was his match at every level.

Except in the kitchen. Which was an entirely different matter.

She curled onto her side, and Mittens found a nest on top of the sheets behind her crooked knees. She heard little licking sounds as the kitten bathed herself, and finally, silence.

At last Allie's eyelids grew heavy and she slept, only to be rudely awakened by an irritating rapping on her door. Mittens flew off the bed as though she had been launched.

"What!" Allie exclaimed.

"Rise and shine, sleepyhead. It's past time to be up and at 'em."

Blurry-eyed, she peered out the window. "The sun is barely up." She never rose at this hour. The servants did, of course, to prepare her morning meal, but she had no intention of—

"Come on, get yourself some breakfast and let's get going if you want to do some shopping in Bridle," Cord said.

Shopping. Now that was a task for which she had a great deal of experience.

She hopped out of bed, grabbed her wrapper and opened the door a crack. "Would you mind bringing me a cup of coffee to sip while I prepare myself for shopping?"

Looking mystified by her request, he leaned a hand on the doorjamb. "Maybe I better clear up something here. In this country, the *housekeeper* fixes coffee and brings a mug to the *boss,* not the other way around."

"Oh. Well, if such a simple request is too difficult for you to perform, then I shall get my own coffee." Pulling her wrapper modestly around her, she flounced past him. Surely he didn't expect her to do any *work* before she had consumed her first cup of coffee.

Cord's jaw went slack, while other parts of his anatomy got an early wake-up call. Sleepy eyed and wearing her hair in a thick braid that hung halfway down her back, Leila was resplendent in an ornate, royal-blue silk gown embroidered in gold and red swirls. Barefooted, so he could see her delicate ankles and arched insteps, she padded from her doorway across the width of the kitchen floor to the coffeepot and poured herself a cup.

Cord didn't know quite what he wanted to do first—slip off Leila's gown and take her back to her bed, where he could explore her slender body, starting with her sexy, shocking-red toenails, or read her the riot act for not behaving like any servant he'd ever met.

Before he could decide, the kitten pounced on his leg, burying her claws in his calf. "Hey, cut that out!"

Coffee mug in hand, Leila sailed by him, snatching the kitten from his leg. "Please do not speak so curtly to Mittens. You will hurt her feelings." Stepping into her room, she closed the door behind her.

Cord opted not to bang his head against the thick adobe wall. It wouldn't do any good. And he sure as hell was likely to hurt himself—or the wall.

But maybe he could bribe Sheikh Rafe with a couple hundred acres of Texas grassland to take Leila back.

The woman acted nothing like the meek servant who had gotten into his truck yesterday at the Desert Rose with the sheikh watching her. The moment they'd been out of sight of the Coleman's place, her subservient mask had slipped.

It made him wonder what game she was playing— and if he was the one being taken for a ride.

THE TOWN OF BRIDLE was little larger than a village in Munir, although Allie conceded the surrounding farmland was more lush and interesting than the date trees and oil derricks of her desert country. While seeking to purchase stock from the Desert Rose, her brother had insisted they stay as close to the horse ranch as they could. The accommodations they found at the Bridle Motel had been barely adequate for their needs.

Allie wondered if the shopping facilities, which she had not had an opportunity to visit, would be any better. Given the small size of the town and the cracked sidewalks, she would have preferred to shop in Austin. Or better yet, in Dallas.

Still, Bridle was quaintly American and right out of the Old West as she'd seen it on television.

Driving with his elbow on the truck's windowsill, Cord asked, "What do you want to do first? Get the forms at the post office or go shopping?"

She smiled at him. "Shopping is always a priority with me."

"Somehow I thought that might be true." He angled the pickup into a spot in front of a Western clothing store. "What kind of duds are you looking to buy?"

"Duds?"

"Clothes. Not ball gowns, I trust."

"Oh, no, I wish to wear clothes like those your sister wears. American jeans. A cowboy hat. Boots. That is what women wear here." *Even out in public,* she thought in amazement. Although some of her countrywomen wore such things in the privacy of their own homes, she had never had that luxury. She had her position to think of, an image to maintain even among the servants. But now she was free to choose clothes on her own. *Temporarily.*

"So you're going whole-hog Western style, huh?"

"Have you heard the expression, when in Rome—"

"I have."

"Then surely it applies in the same way when in Texas."

"I believe it does, Leila." His amused smile sent her heart fluttering. "I believe it does."

Once inside the store, Cord hung back while Leila circled the merchandise like a pack of coyotes picking out a weak heifer to attack. She fingered jeans and shirts, tried on hats, examined leather boots, looking as though at any moment she was going to close in for the kill.

Sherianne Wilcox, a teenager from one of the nearby farms who worked part-time at the store, walked over to Cord.

"Can I help you find something, Mr. Brannigan?"

"Nope. I'm just waiting for the young lady to make up her mind."

The teenager glanced toward Leila. "She's real pretty."

"That she is." Leila had whipped her long hair into a knot that rested at her nape, a target a man would aim for with a kiss. And then he'd untie that knot, letting her hair stream through his fingers.

"Is she your girlfriend?"

He jolted at Sherianne's question, yanking his attention back to the youngster. "Nope. Housekeeper."

The girl's eyes widened in surprise, her smile revealing a shiny set of braces. "Well, she's sure lots purdier than Maria is."

Despite the air-conditioning, heat raced up Cord's neck. "I'll just go see how she's coming along."

He jammed his hands in his pockets and strolled to the back of the store. By now, Leila had gathered an armload of clothes and had a totally impractical white Stetson perched on her head.

"You about done here?" he asked.

"I need to try these on to see if they fit. Then I will be ready to go with you."

"Okay, but I've got to get back to the ranch sometime this year. Can you move it along a little faster?"

She did that funny toss of her head thing, suggesting she'd do as she pleased, then vanished into a dressing room.

Little wonder men didn't like to go shopping with women. When he needed a pair of jeans, he came into the store, picked out a pair of 32-34s, paid for 'em and was done with it. Leila was making a damn career out of this shopping trip.

He checked his watch, then paced around the store. Obviously her view of shopping—and his view of work—were in direct conflict.

"What do you think, Cord?"

He turned and got what amounted to a visual punch in the solar plexus. Standing in front of the arched doorway to the dressing room, she took his breath away. Like a fashion model, she pirouetted in a full circle so he could get a good look. She'd picked out a tank top that bared her arms and dipped low toward her delicate breasts, then tucked in at her narrow waist. Her jeans were as snug as tights, molding to her attractive rear end like a man's hand. The expensive leather boots made her legs look like they went on forever.

He cleared his throat. "Great. You look like a Dallas Cowboys cheerleader."

"This cheerleader business is good?"

"Very good." For her. Or the football team. Very *bad* for Cord, if he had any hope of keeping his hands to himself and his head on straight. "So, you're ready to go, huh?"

"Oh, no. I have many more outfits to try on."

He rolled his eyes. Thank goodness his men were more than capable of separating the calves from their mothers in order to wean them. At the rate Leila was going, they wouldn't get back to the ranch until past dinnertime.

Allie made her selections, and with her arms full of clothes, stepped out of the dressing room. Cord ushered her to the cash register with ill-disguised impatience. He really needed to develop more regard for a woman's need to dress appropriately, whatever her role in life. Even a servant wanted to look nice.

She placed the clothing and boots on the counter, topping the pile with her bright new Western hat.

"Will that be cash or credit card?" the young woman asked.

Allie stared at her blankly for a moment. Dear heaven! She'd left her Visa card at the ranch, but even if she'd brought it along she wouldn't have been able to use it, not if she had to sign her real name—Aliah Bahram. And she certainly didn't carry enough cash with her to pay for all of this. In Munir, she purchased whatever caught her eye. Either a servant paid for it or the merchant sent the bill to the palace—for Rafe to grumble over and eventually pay.

Sensing her dilemma, Cord stepped up to the cash register. "Charge it to the Flying Ace account. They're sort of her work clothes." He gestured vaguely to the mountain of clothes on the counter. If nothing else, it seemed as if the only way he'd get back to the Flying Ace in this century would be to pay for the goods himself.

Leila wasn't a woman who could be easily denied anything she wanted. He didn't have the time or inclination to argue with her.

A few minutes later, feeling like a pack mule, he carried a half-dozen sacks out to the truck, squeezing them behind the seat.

"Do you want to get the forms from the post office now?" he ask.

"I think I am too weary to deal with so many details right now. Perhaps another day."

Right. He was happy to put off that ordeal, too. "How 'bout lunch before we head home?"

She brightened. "Yes, that would be nice. If I don't have to prepare the meal," she qualified.

"My treat." His finances had already taken a big whack. A few more bucks at the local diner wouldn't hurt him, and maybe the delighted smile she gave him was worth it.

Man, he was losing it. Big time.

By the time he'd consumed half of his burger and

fries—and Leila had daintily eaten about a quarter of a Cobb salad—Cord asked, "How is it your accent sounds British?"

"It does?" Looking surprised, she stabbed a bite of ham with her fork and chewed thoughtfully. "I suppose it is because my tutor was from England."

Taking another bite of burger, he studied her a minute. "You mean your sheikh boss hires tutors for his servants?"

Her head snapped up. "Oh, no, not that. I meant, my *mistress's* tutor was from England. I was permitted to sit in on her lessons."

"Ah, I see." Something about the flare of color on her cheeks suggested she wasn't telling the entire truth, though he couldn't figure out why she'd lie. "Guess we Texans sound different to you."

"Not unpleasantly so." She smiled again, and he lost track of what he'd been puzzling over a minute ago.

Not that it mattered. According to Brianna, with only a tourist visa Leila would have to go home soon. That was fine by Cord. He wasn't sure how much more strain the fly of his jeans could take.

ALLIE STEPPED BACK from her closet to admire her newly purchased wardrobe, which she'd hung with great delight. Studying the array of jeans and tank tops, cotton blouses and denim skirts, she gnawed on her lower lip. She'd spent extravagantly for clothing her betrothed husband would never approve of her wearing. Her throat tightened at that reality. She had so little time to enjoy her liberty before being forced back into the role demanded of a princess.

The kitten wove her way between Allie's feet, meowing.

Allie scooped her up. "What is it, my precious Mittens? Are you hungry?" Fortunately, she had thought to have Cord stop at the grocery store in Bridle to buy cat food on their way home. He'd also wisely purchased a precooked roasted chicken for their evening meal.

She carried Mittens into the kitchen, found a dish and opened the box of cat food.

Coming through the open window, the racket of ranch operations seemed inordinately loud. Cows were bawling and carrying on as though they were in great distress.

Allie looked up from pouring the cat food when Cord walked into the room, hooking his Stetson on a peg near the doorway.

"Why are the cows so upset?" she asked.

"It's weaning time. It takes a couple of days for the heifers' milk to dry up, and they miss their calves. Same thing for the calves."

"You have separated the mothers and their babies?" she gasped.

"Have to. Most of the heifers are pregnant again and they need their strength for their next calf."

"But that is so cruel." Allie remembered the night following her mother's death. She had thought her own heart would break. While visiting some of the poorer villages in Munir, hoping to improve the conditions in which her people lived, Allie's mother had contracted a dreadful disease. Day by day she had wasted away, the doctors unable to help. And then she had simply stopped breathing. Allie had wanted to die, too.

"Leila." He shoved his fingers through his sweat-dampened hair. "This is a working ranch, not a zoo or a pet farm. We raise animals that are turned into steaks and short ribs and rump roasts, and we do it as efficiently as we can. The calves are old enough to graze on their own and their mothers do better this way."

He left her standing in the kitchen puzzling over his words. From the sound the cows were making, Allie did not believe Cord that all was as it should be. And when she stepped outside, she knew she was right. From the porch she could see the first pasture where calves were lined up on one side of the fence, cows on the other, desperately trying to get to each other.

Tears blurred her vision as memories of her mother swept over her, memories of loss. "Poor babies. I wish I could help you."

BY EVENING, the racket had increased in volume. Neither Cord nor Brianna seemed disturbed by the noise. But it set Allie's teeth on edge and gave her a dreadful headache.

In bed, she covered her ears with a pillow. Nothing blocked out the noise—or the image of herself as a five-year-old child, sobbing uncontrollably with no one to hold her, to tell her all would be well.

At her mother's funeral, Allie's father and brother had been clear-eyed and strong. They'd told her she must be, too. But she could not help herself. She'd failed, shaming her family, and was sent to the women's quarters alone.

So alone…

Gasping for air, she sat up. Sweat edged down her neck and between her breasts. She could not endure the racket, the pain of those poor animals.

Tugging on jeans and her new boots, she hurried out into the darkness of night. No one had been there to console her when she had needed it. The least she could do was help these poor helpless animals.

No matter what Cord had said.

Chapter Four

Cord woke with a start.

The sun wasn't up yet. Only predawn light slipped past the lace curtains on the windows. The air was cool, with a trace of rain that had fallen during the night.

After nearly thirty-five years of living on the Flying Ace, Cord knew every sound made on the ranch. The creak of the house as it settled. Movement in the kitchen that meant someone was up fixing coffee or a snack. The soft patter of rain on the flower beds outside or the silence that came with a rare snowfall. Even the dreaded roar of an approaching tornado.

As a kid he used to lie in his bed down the hallway, listening to his parents fight here in the master bedroom. He'd put his head under the pillow, pretending everything was okay. It wasn't. He'd known that because the next morning his mother's eyes were always red from crying.

Right now he didn't hear anything out of the ordinary, but he knew something was wrong—knew it from the way the hair stood up at the back of his neck.

He got up and pulled on some clothes, not bothering to tuck in his shirt.

Down the hall, Brianna's door was still shut. No sound came from the office or any other room on this side of the house.

The living room looked a little dusty and unused. The kitchen was as they had left it last night, the faint hint of leftover chicken in the air. Just off the kitchen, the door to the housekeeper's room where Leila slept was closed tight. Still, something didn't feel right.

Stepping outside, he drew in a breath of morning air. Everything looked and smelled all right. No smoke rising from the barn. No twister approaching on the horizon. His cows and their calves grazing quietly in the home pasture, the gate between—

"Damn!" he muttered.

Turning on his heel, he marched toward the bunkhouse. He didn't tolerate carelessness, and whoever had left the gate open had cost him and his men a day's worth of work.

He rapped hard on the bunkhouse door before shoving it open. "Good morning, gentlemen."

They stirred, coming awake slowly. "Hey, boss," Pablo mumbled.

"Anybody want to tell me who forgot to latch the gate in the home pasture last night?"

Wearing only his skivvies, Red threw his legs over the side of his bunk and scrubbed the sleep from his face. "How come you're askin'?"

"The calves got back into the main pasture."

All five men looked at each other.

Pablo, who pretty much handled the role of foreman, said, "I checked the gate, boss. Last thing I did before calling it a night. It was locked up tight when we came in for supper."

Cord had never had any reason to doubt Pablo's word before. But if one of the men hadn't left the gate unlatched, who would have—?

He cursed under his breath. He had a pretty good idea what had happened, and his hired hands weren't at fault, at least not those who lived in the bunkhouse.

"Looks like we'll have to separate the calves again, boys. Sorry 'bout that. Move the whole herd over to the east pasture and keep 'em apart there this time." Farther away from the ranch house, a longer walk for little Miss Mischief, if his second guess about the culprit was right.

Just to make sure this time, he strolled out into the pasture, talking softly to the animals so they wouldn't spook. After the rain the air smelled fresh, and the heat of day hadn't raised the humidity yet. In the damp ground beside the gate were telltale prints made by a set of size six woman's boots. He knew the size because he'd paid for them.

That woman was really getting on his nerves. Not only was he thinking heated thoughts he shouldn't be having, she was creating extra work for his men. That really had to stop.

He walked back to the ranch house and, to his surprise, found Leila in the kitchen, fully dressed, making coffee. The striped black-and-brown kitten was mewling around her feet, looking for her breakfast.

None of which reduced his annoyance one whit.

"Just what did you think you were doing?"

She whirled around, almost dropping the tin of coffee. "I am making coffee. Is that not what you wish?"

"I'm talking about last night when you opened the gate so the calves could get to their mothers."

"That was a cruel thing you did, separating them." She turned her back on him and resumed putting grounds in the coffeemaker.

In two steps, he'd reached her, touched her arm.

She spun back to him, startled and defensive.

"Now, you listen to me, Mischief. My men are going to have redo everything they did yesterday. Moving cattle, particularly calves, is hot, dirty and sometimes dangerous work. You are not to mess with anything to do with the workings of this ranch again, do you understand me?"

She looked up at him with wide eyes, all dark and gleaming. He was close enough to catch her tropical scent of jasmine, and her arm beneath his hand felt fragile, her flesh smooth and caressable.

Suddenly, tears pooled in her eyes and one spilled down her pale cheek. "I'm s-sorry."

Afraid he'd hurt her, he let go as if he'd been scalded. "Look, I didn't mean to—"

"I felt so sorry for the babies to lose their mothers as I lost mine. I didn't think it would hurt, one night—"

"You lost your mother?"

"A long time ago, when I was just a little girl." A sob shuddered through her. "They had this big funeral for her and they were going to put her in the ground. I knew she did not like the dark, and they told me I should not cry. I could not help myself."

With his thumb, he wiped the tear from her cheek. "And that's why you unlatched the gate."

She nodded, though her chin trembled. "It did not seem like such an awful thing to do. Not for the cows, at any rate. They were happy with what I did."

He couldn't argue with that logic. It just wasn't the way a rancher looked at things. A rancher had to be tough. He didn't cry. He didn't make a fuss over cows and their calves being separated. That was life.

"You don't know much about raising horses or cattle, do you?"

Her eyes still pooled with tears, she shook her head. "I was only allowed to ride, never to care for the animals. It was not permitted."

"Come over here and sit down a minute." He led her to the kitchen table, pulled out a chair for her. He wanted to console her, take her in his arms. But that didn't seem like a good plan. She was his employee, of sorts. And he doubted he'd be able to stop holding her once he started.

He knew he'd made the right decision when Brianna picked that moment to walk into the kitchen.

"Good morning. You're both up early." Her gaze took in the two of them sitting at the table, then swung around to the empty pot of coffee. "Did you want me to finish fixing the coffee?"

"I would have completed my task, but your bully of a brother has interrupted my duties to chastise me for what I have done."

Brianna's blond brows pulled together in surprise. "Cord..."

Shoving back his chair, he stood. "Wait a minute, ladies. Brianna, if you wouldn't mind, could you make the coffee? Meanwhile, Leila and I are going to step into my office to have a serious discussion about her employment."

"Sure," Brianna said with a shrug, her eyes still filled with curiosity and a hint of censure.

"Leila?" He gestured toward his office in the other wing of the house. "After you."

"First you tell me one thing and then you tell me another," she protested. But she had little choice but to do as he ordered.

Cord was getting the darndest feeling he'd been duped. No servant anywhere in the universe would act as Leila had, knowing his intentions and virtually disobeying a direct order about the calves, talking back to him. It didn't make any sense.

Unless Leila wasn't a servant at all, but a *princess*.

Princess Allie, who was engaged to be married to some wealthy, well-connected man in her homeland at a ceremony the entire population would help to celebrate, according to Sheikh Rafe.

But why the hell would a princess masquerade as

a servant? Go so far as to agree to being a house-keeper when she didn't know squat about the job?

Whatever was going on, he intended to call her bluff. If she really was a princess, she wouldn't agree to his terms. Unless she had a helluva good reason not to go back to Munir.

Suddenly he remembered the sheikh's subtle threat of punishment—that he'd make amends if his "servant" didn't measure up. Damn! The man wouldn't harm his own sister, would he?

When they reached his office, Cord said, "Sit down, Leila, if that's really your name."

Her head jerked up. "I am Leila, as I have said."

Maybe. He was used to ramrodding a crew of cowhands, giving orders. But it went against his nature to bully a woman. Still, something didn't wash here, and he didn't know any other way to get to the truth.

"Whoever you are, you agreed to work as my housekeeper. My offer to send you back to Munir is still open, but if you decide to stay here there are going to be some changes."

"As you wish," she said tautly.

"Everyone on this ranch carries their fair share of the workload. You haven't been. From now on, things will be different.

"In your case, that means that you cook the meals, clean up afterwards, do the washing, vacuuming. Clean the bathrooms, including the toilets. Wash windows. Whatever a housekeeper usually does, from now on that's your job."

She paled considerably, making Cord feel rotten.

Hell, he'd never even ordered Maria to do those things. She just did them; she knew what was expected of her. Which was the crux of the problem. Leila didn't seem to know she was a servant. And he didn't like running roughshod over her any more than she appeared to be enjoying it.

"And just to make sure you understand my position, I'm going to start you off this morning with Maria's favorite job. You're going to gather the eggs from the hens, then clean the chicken coop."

"You can't mean—" Allie's hand flew to her mouth. How could she possibly do all that he asked of her?

"It's my way, or you can start packing your bags for the trip back to Munir. You've got ten seconds to decide."

He stood above her, his arms folded across his chest, his golden-green eyes filled with self-righteousness, much the same way her brother looked at her. *The bully!* He was trying to get rid of her. Well, she didn't give up easily.

She lifted her chin. Her time to return to Munir had not yet come. Her brother had not yet discovered her absence or he would have come back for her.

And Rafe would hand her over to Sardar Bin Douri the moment their plane touched down at the capital city of Jada. She could expect little kindness or understanding from her betrothed. Theirs would be a marriage based on a business arrangement and political influence.

She shuddered and pressed her lips together.

Mittens scampered into the office and jumped into her lap, curling up there, purring and wanting to be petted. Who would care for her kitten if she was sent back to Munir?

Allie's throat tightened, but she forced herself to speak. "I agree to your terms." With Mittens in her arms and her head held high, mustering every bit of pride she had, she stood and left the office.

Watching her leave, Cord wondered if he had miscalculated. He'd thought for sure the threat of the chicken coop would make her show her true colors. A *princess* wouldn't stoop that low. Hell, most *servants* would tell him to find somebody else to do his dirty work.

He followed her toward the kitchen, but she was already gone. Brianna was making herself some toast. She'd brewed the coffee and he poured himself a cup.

"That was an interesting scene I interrupted. What's going on?" Brianna asked.

Leaning back against the counter, he sipped the hot coffee. It burned clear down his throat, but was no less painful than the guilt churning in his gut. "She's going to clean the chicken coop."

Brianna raised her brows. "You're making her do that?"

"I gave her the choice of that or going back home. She picked the chicken coop."

"Heavens, if you'd made me clean that smelly thing, I would have headed on back to New Hampshire in a heartbeat."

"I don't know, sis. You can be pretty stubborn when you set your mind to something."

"But the chicken coop?" She shook her head, her blond ponytail swinging gently from side to side. "Now, *that's* being stubborn. I think I could learn to like Leila."

If she was Leila, not a runaway princess. He very much suspected it was the latter.

ALLIE GAGGED at the horrible smell in the chicken coop and fought the bile that rose in her throat. She would *not* quit. But at this point, only pride kept her going.

That and a noisy rooster that kept egging her on. Or maybe he was protecting his pretty little hens on their nests. Although Allie needed protection more than they did. While she was gathering eggs, *two* of the wicked beasts had pecked at her hand, drawing blood.

She rubbed the bloody back of her hand on her filthy jeans. She supposed she might do the same as the hens if someone was trying to steal *her* babies.

"Mr. Rooster, you are full of pride—and a bully like your master."

He crowed loudly, then scratched at the dirt near Allie's muddy boots.

Wiping the sweat from her forehead with her forearm, she hefted the shovel one more time. Her back ached, her palms stung, but she wasn't beaten yet. Not when she considered the alternative.

One of the ranch hands stepped into the coop and tipped his hat. "Howdy there, Miss Leila."

"Hello, Joe. If you are looking for eggs, I have already gathered them from their nests."

"No, ma'am, it's not eggs I'm after." An embarrassed blush rose up his neck, turning his age-weathered face a bright red. "I saw you workin' in here and thought you might need a helping hand."

"You want to help me?"

He took the shovel from her. "Wouldn't mind. 'Sides, a purdy little filly like you shouldn't be workin' so hard on such a hot day."

"Cord told me I must. I would not want him to think I am a shirker."

"Aw, shucks, Miss Leila, nobody would think that of you." Impossibly, his face turned an even brighter red, and he leaned into the shovel, scooping a shovelful of the unpleasant mess into the wheelbarrow she had found in the barn.

The rooster crowed in displeasure at the new arrival, and the sitting hens clucked in agreement, some of them flying up to perch on a beam near the ceiling.

A moment later, Ty arrived with his own shovel. "Thought I'd lend a hand, iff'n you don't mind," he drawled, touching his fingertips to the brim of his hat before getting down to work.

Allie stepped aside when Red showed up with an empty wheelbarrow, smiling shyly, and took the full one off to an unknown destination.

What sweet men—unlike her employer, she thought with pleasure.

CORD SPOTTED A COUPLE of his cowhands' horses in the corral, but no sign of his men. They must have finished separating the calves early, he mused. He was about to saddle his own mount, planning to ride out to the east pasture, when he heard talking from the direction of the chicken coop.

Puzzled, he strolled in that direction, stopping in the shade of the barn.

Miss Mischief was up to her tricks again. Sitting on a wooden crate, she was holding court with his hired hands as the audience. They shoveled while she chattered on about riding a camel across the desert of Munir to an oasis that had the sweetest water imaginable and the tastiest dates picked right from the tree. The way she told the tale, any one of his hired hands would sign on for a trip with her to that oasis—or anywhere else, for that matter—at the drop of a Stetson. She had an amazing presence that made a man want to do whatever she asked of him—as though she were a princess expecting nothing less than total devotion.

Cord was no exception, just a little more determined to not let her wrap him around her little finger. He didn't like the possibility that she was here on a fling, slumming, using him like a dumb Texas cowboy—as Sandra Maddox had done.

To Leila's credit, she'd obviously done some of the grungy work herself. Dirt streaked her face; her jeans and new boots were filthy. Cord would venture a guess that she'd sweated more in the past couple of hours than she had in her entire lifetime.

All of which made him feel damn guilty for forcing her to put up or get back on a plane to Munir.

Why the hell *hadn't* she opted for the trip back home when he'd offered it? Was she *scared* to go back? Did she think he'd throw her to the lions, if that was what was happening? If she'd just tell him the truth...

Not wanting to embarrass her or his men—or maybe it was his sense of guilt—he backed away from the scene, went to the stables and saddled a horse. He'd check on the herd. Cattle were a lot easier to understand than a woman, and not anywhere near as disturbing to his libido.

EVERY BONE IN ALLIE'S body ached, the palms of her hands were so abraded no amount of lotion could soothe them, and dinner had been a disaster. She'd tried to cook hamburgers on the indoor grill. She'd barely avoided catching her hair on fire, the smoke alarm had gone off and the hamburger patties, resembling volcanic rocks, were barely palatable.

They had all eaten in grim silence until Allie asked, "Do you have a computer with access to the Internet?"

Cord and Brianna had glanced at each other. "Sure," Cord said.

"May I have your permission to use your computer?"

"You know how to use a computer?"

His surprise offended her. "Munir is both a wealthy and a technologically advanced country. Of course I do.'' Not that she was an expert, but she certainly knew how to shop via the Internet. Which was what she intended to do to prevent them all from starving or suffering food poisoning due to her dismal culinary efforts.

So now she sat at Brianna's desk, using her computer, with Mittens curled on top of the monitor. Allie busily clicked through sources for exotic foods and recipes. If she couldn't cook American food, which was unfamiliar to her, she could perhaps learn to prepare meals like those she'd eaten every day of her life.

While she worked, she was fiercely aware of Cord sitting at his desk across the room from her. But she didn't look in his direction. She didn't want him to know just how nervous he made her feel, how edgy and flushed she became whenever they were in the same room together.

How much she wanted to please him.

FOR AN HOUR, Cord had been pretending to study the reproductive history of the bulls to be auctioned at Austin next week. The bulls couldn't hold a candle to the way Leila held his attention across the room. From where he sat—unable to see the screen—it looked as though she knew her way around the Internet.

Unless she was e-mailing friends at home with a plea to get her out of Texas.

Except she was printing out stuff, too. He had no idea what.

He cleared his throat. "Are you finding whatever you need?"

"Yes, thank you." She kept her eyes focused on the monitor, ignoring him.

He shuffled the papers around on his desk. He wasn't neat at keeping his business records. Fortunately, Brianna had reduced the piles of paperwork he'd always had on his desk to a manageable size.

"I checked out the chicken coop. You did a really good job cleaning it up."

Her head snapped up, and what he suspected was a guilty blush tinged her sculpted cheekbones. "I did?"

"It's never looked better. Thanks."

Averting her gaze, she breathed, "Some of your men helped me."

He smiled at her coming clean about her devoted crew of volunteers. If he hadn't wandered over to the chicken coop at just the right time, she could have gotten away with a fib, let him think she'd done all the work herself. Which would have made him feel even more guilty than he already did about making her clean up the mess.

"It's okay, Mischief. The work got done, and that's what matters. As long as the men get their work done, too."

"Why do you call me 'Mischief'?"

"Because somehow you manage to disrupt the whole ranch just by being here. Besides, you don't want me to call you Princess."

Her chocolate-brown eyes widened, and she

quickly looked down at her hands, rubbing her thumb over her palm. "No, I do not want that."

Another stab of guilt punched him in the gut. "Did you get blisters today?"

"A few, perhaps."

He cursed himself for not having thought to get her some gloves. Whoever she was, princess or servant, she wasn't used to manual labor. That much was obvious. "I've got some ointment that will take the sting out." He rummaged in the back of the desk drawer for the little silver tube he knew was there, finally finding it mashed into the farthest corner.

Shoving back from the desk, the leather chair protesting the sudden movement with a groan of its aging springs, Cord crossed the room and hunkered down next to Leila.

"Let's see how bad your hands are."

"I used some lotion—"

"This stuff is better. Works wonders. You'll see."

His hand dwarfed hers as he examined the abrasions on her palm, his fingers rough and scarred compared to the milky softness of her skin. Her tapered fingers looked fragile next to his. The bones too fine, the skin too sensitive to grip a shovel.

He rubbed a drop of the ointment into her palm, soothing the streak of chafed skin. He remembered as a kid visiting a carnival, having his palm read. He would have a long life, the fortune teller had said, and one true love. He'd laughed at that. Twelve-year-olds whose mothers had run off had no interest in love and only a mild curiosity about girls.

The latter feeling had changed over time, but not the former—with one brief exception, which he'd paid for dearly.

Despite that, as he traced Leila's lifeline, angled from wrist to middle finger, he couldn't help but wonder what it would be like to grow old with her. Days filled with surprises, he imagined, and nights consumed by the passion he sensed shimmered right below the surface whenever he looked at her. Her stubbornness would challenge a man, her empathy for farm creatures drive him crazy.

But the nights would provide the reward for his patience. His own special princess, because he was having more and more trouble thinking of her as anyone's servant.

Princess Aliah Bahram. Allie, whether she wanted him to call her that or not. The name fit. Still, there was no way he could be one hundred percent sure.

Perched on top of the monitor, Mittens grew restless. She stretched, yawned, then hopped down, treading daintily across the keyboard before jumping to the floor.

Cord paid the kitten no attention, concentrating instead on the smooth flesh of Allie's palm beneath his fingertips.

When he finished applying the ointment to the second palm, he looked up. She'd bent over to watch while he worked, bringing her lips within inches of his. Their shape was perfectly symmetrical, the dip in the middle of her upper lip temptingly close. Their taste would be as sweet as milk chocolate, but with the bite of mulishness. A fascinating combination.

For the sake of his ego, he supposed, if she was the princess he *needed* her to trust him.

"Does that feel better, Allie?"

Her gaze was focused on his mouth, her eyes dilated with the first hint of arousal. "Much better. Thank you." She whispered the words, her voice low and husky, then blinked as she realized what he had said.

Abruptly, she pushed herself away. "First you call me Mischief and then by the name of my mistress. Do you not know by now that I am Leila, your housekeeper?"

He backed away, too, and stood. Her hot denial that she was the princess didn't fool Cord. She'd responded too quickly, too naturally to the name Allie, flushing when she realized what she'd done.

He didn't know why she wanted to remain incognito, and he didn't much like playing her game. Sandra Maddox had turned him into a sucker, using him as a cover for her clandestine affair with a married man.

Cord wasn't going to go that route again.

The one thing he demanded of a woman these days was complete honesty. His instincts told him he wasn't getting it from Leila.

And as long as she kept the truth from him, he'd keep his hands off, no matter how tempting she was. Or willing, despite her engagement to another man.

"Tell me." He leaned back against his desk,

crossing his ankles and resting his hands beside him. Only the flex of his jaw would give away the tension that was still surging through him. "What's the man like who, uh, your mistress is supposed to marry?"

Her eyes grew wary. "Why do you ask?"

"Let's just say I'm a curious kind of guy." One who had a particular affinity for the truth when it came to women.

"He is old."

"How old? Sixty? Seventy?"

"No, not that old. Perhaps forty. Maybe a little more."

"Great. You're making me feel ancient. I'm thirty-five."

"Yes, but you are—" she hesitated, and he indicated she should continue "—robust. And kind, when you are not being a bully."

His lips twitched at the miserly compliment. *Robust.* An interesting description. "So I take it she doesn't want to marry such an old geezer."

"He also has hair growing out of his ears and his nose."

"I certainly wouldn't want to marry a woman like that."

"You are mocking me. Sardar Bin Douri is not a nice man."

The force with which she condemned the man to whom she—or her mistress—was engaged got Cord's attention. "What do you mean by not nice?"

She glanced away, unable to meet his gaze. Mittens returned from wherever she'd been, licking her chops, and jumped into the her lap. Idly, she stroked the kitten's head, apparently unaware of what a maternal image she presented.

"There are rumors," she said. "Servants talk among themselves. Sardar's wife died a year ago. They had been married for many years, yet she had never given him a son."

"That happens sometimes."

Still petting the kitten, Leila looked up at Cord. "It is said his wife was very afraid of the water, would not set foot on even a large yacht. Still, she went out on a small motorboat alone with her husband. She never came back. He said she fell off the boat and drowned."

"Are you saying he killed her?"

"No one knows. But what if I…what if my mistress cannot give him a son?" A sudden sheen of tears appeared in her eyes, making them glisten. "What will become of her?"

Something resembling a knife twisted in Cord's gut. Maybe Allie had a damn good reason to stay in Texas.

"Why would Princess Aliah's brother force her to marry a man like that?"

"Bin Douri has a great deal of money. Almost as much as the sheikh. And he controls the pipelines through which the sheikh's oil must flow, plus owns the tankers that carry the oil to market."

"Then this marriage is a business deal cementing the relationship."

"Yes." Fear of Bin Douri—and fear of being unmasked—caused Allie to squeeze Mittens too tightly. The kitten meowed, bolting from her lap. Her hands trembled.

If only she could read Cord's heart. In her country, if a man discovered her masquerade, he would return her immediately to her brother for fear of political repercussions. The sheikh's influence was powerful and so was Bin Douri's.

She knew America was different and far from Munir. But Cord's neighbors were conducting business with Rafe; the Coleman family might urge him to send her home even if he didn't wish to do so himself.

Men, it seemed to her, always stuck together.

Despite his suspicions, she dared not tell Cord the truth. Not yet. Not until she had no other choice.

Yet it was her own heart that troubled her the most. The yearning she had felt as he caressed her palms. Her desperate urge to place her lips on his.

To experience for the first time a man's kiss.

Chapter Five

Two days later, Airborne Express delivered sixteen packages to the Flying Ace.

"What's going on?" Cord asked the delivery man as he hauled stuff up onto the porch.

"Don't worry about a thing, Mr. Brannigan. It's all taken care of."

Allie scurried out the front door, picking up a couple of boxes and carrying them back inside. Her kitten bounded past her, escaping through the open door to explore the outside world.

A feeling of unease edged down Cord's spine. The Airborne guy might think everything was okay, but he wasn't so sure.

He picked up a box marked PERISHABLE in big letters and followed his housekeeper into the kitchen.

"Hey, Mischief, what's going on?"

"Dinner," she replied succinctly, before heading back to the front porch again.

It was before noon, well before dinnertime, and Airborne Express wasn't noted for it's take-out deliveries, as far as Cord knew.

He studied the boxes Allie had already brought in. Since most of the labels were in Arabic, he didn't get much of a clue as to their contents.

As she whizzed past him again, he said, "Who's paying for all this stuff?"

"The Flying Ace, of course."

"Now wait a minute!" He snared her by the arm, the first time he'd touched her since the night he'd applied ointment to her hand. A jolt as potent as that delivered by an electric fence whipped through him, which he tried to ignore. "You can't, willy-nilly, go around charging whatever you want to my account. Speaking of which, how did you get my number?"

"It was on the receipt for the work clothes you purchased for me."

She twisted away from him and propped her fist on her hip, glaring at him. She was wearing a strappy T-shirt with her jeans and her face glowed with a fine sheen of sweat. Her breasts weren't very big, so she probably didn't need a bra. But damned if Cord didn't wish she was wearing one, anyway. The swell of her small breasts, her puckered nipples, were too tempting by far. And distracting. For a moment, he couldn't recall why she was shooting daggers at him. Probably emerald-studded ones.

"What has been delivered is for your dinner the next several days. Since I cannot cook hamburgers, as you may have noticed, I will prepare other meals. Ones you will find even more tasty than bland ground meat on a bun, I assure you. And I cannot purchase the appropriate ingredients at the Bridle grocery store, so I ordered the necessary spices and meats, et cetera, on the Internet." She huffed imperiously and marched out of the kitchen to retrieve another load of boxes.

Damn, he never should have allowed her access to the ranch's computer. Or to American-style clothing, for that matter. He'd been better off with her totally covered in a cloak and veil.

Now his only recourse was to take cold showers— a lot of them.

When she had all the boxes stacked up on the table, she gave him the evil eye again.

"On this big ranch you can find nothing to do?" she asked.

"I've got plenty to do—"

"Then if you wish me to prepare your dinner, please find yourself somewhere else to do it."

He stifled a grin. He had to give her points for spunk. Unlike a lot of women, she didn't know the meaning of *fawn.* Or *humility,* for that matter. But in a strange way her attitude was refreshing. Nobody was going to push her around.

Which made the things she was doing—like cleaning the chicken coop—all the more amazing, because he suspected another woman in her position would simply walk away.

After he left the kitchen, grabbing an apple on the way out to have for lunch, she practically barricaded herself inside. He saw nothing of her all afternoon, although there was an occasional clatter of pots and pans. Finally, toward dinnertime, the rich scent of meat and spices wafted out onto the patio where Cord and Brianna waited.

"What do you think she's up to?" he asked. He stared at the closed door, all but willing it to open.

"I don't know, but it certainly smells interesting," Brianna said.

A tile fountain bubbled in the center of the Spanish-style patio, water splashing softly, the mist cooling the air. Normally the sound soothed Cord. But not tonight. Instead, he paced around the patio like a caged animal.

"Relax, Cord. She'll call us in to dinner soon."

"Damnedest thing, not being allowed to go into my own kitchen when I want to." Spunk could be carried too far.

Brianna looked cool and unconcerned. "She's probably nervous and doesn't want you checking on her."

He sent his sister a sharp look. "If the past is any example, she's likely to burn down the whole house with her cooking. She needs checking on."

"I think tonight's going to be different."

He muttered a skeptical sound and jammed his fingertips into his hip pockets. A man would be a damn fool to expect any kind of cooking from a princess. Or a palace servant who was used to drawing her mistress's bath, for God's sake.

"How much longer is Maria going to be gone?" he asked.

"You'll have to survive without her for a few more weeks. Her daughter had a hard delivery, and her older children are still hardly more than babies themselves. She's going to need lots of help.''

"Great." His stomach growled. If the meal was bad enough, he supposed he could drive into Bridle for something decent to eat.

The patio door opened. Cord groaned at the sight of Miss Mischief. Her cheeks were flushed. Damp strands of dark hair had escaped the coiled knot at her nape and clung to the slender column of her neck. Unidentifiable stains decorated the front of her strappy T-shirt, visible evidence of her inexperience as a cook. In contrast, her red toenails and bare feet tantalized him.

He'd never seen a more sexy, alluring woman in his life. Which was about the craziest thought he'd ever had.

"Dinner is ready," she announced, then vanished back inside.

Brianna glanced at him. "Give her credit for trying."

He'd be smarter to take her back to the Desert Rose and tell them Allie—or whoever she was—was *their* problem, not his.

The kitchen was a hundred ten degrees. Every pot they owned was on the stove or stacked soaking in the sink. The table had been set, the plates already in place, filled with individual servings.

"Everything smells wonderful," Brianna said, taking her usual seat.

"Thank you. The recipes are from my homeland."

Cord eyed the meal suspiciously. A green lump

filled one corner of his plate. Something that looked like mashed potatoes but clearly wasn't filled another. The meat was recognizable, sort of, although it didn't look like beef, and there was a side dish resembling soggy french fries covered in who-knew-what kind of creamy sauce.

"You want to tell me what all this is? Or am I better off not knowing?"

"Cord!" Brianna warned.

"Do not worry yourself, Brianna. He is like a spoiled child, afraid to try new things."

"I am not—"

"This is *sarma*." She pointed to the green lump. "A very popular dish in my country and very tedious to make."

"Rice stuffed in grape leaves," Brianna explained.

"You're right," Cord muttered. "I don't remember seeing any grape leaves at the grocery store in Bridle."

Allie sniffed with disdain and indicated the white mashed stuff. "This is hummus, made of chickpeas. The meat is lamb, flavored with cinnamon and allspice."

"Lamb in cattle country?" he questioned, but not too harshly. He could see she was proud of her efforts. He could only hope it tasted as good to a Texas palate as it apparently did to an Arab. "And the side dish?"

"Broiled eggplant with garlic and yogurt. We have a pudding for dessert."

Cord had a sudden urge for steak and fries.

Brianna started with the *sarma*. "Umm, this is delicious. Where did you get the grape leaves?"

"There's an Internet site with exotic foods."

While they talked about what went into *sarma*, Cord tried the lamb. He chewed thoughtfully, not quite able to identify the spices she'd used. But the meat was tender, the flavors, a fascinating combination, teasing his tongue.

Exotic compared to an ordinary steak.

He smiled at Allie and her gaze held his, her dark eyes seeking his approval. Her taste, he realized, would be equally exotic and thoroughly enchanting.

"It's good." He looked at her steadily while forking another bite into his mouth, all the while thinking about the new flavors she could introduce him to, the rare combination of sweet innocence and spice that made up her personality.

Tastes that were off-limits to him if she was engaged to another man.

THE STRAIN OF PREPARING and serving dinner had taken its toll on Allie, and she was grateful for Brianna's help cleaning up the kitchen. She had also gained new respect for the servants who prepared meals at the palace.

Standing at the kitchen sink, Brianna was up to her elbows in soapy water, scrubbing the array of pots and pans Allie had dirtied.

Allie picked up a clean towel to dry the pots. "I am surprised you do not mind such work as washing dishes."

Brianna chuckled. ''From the time I was nine or so, I always did the dishes at my aunt's house. And she didn't have a dishwasher.''

''Your aunt? You did not live here with your parents?''

Rinsing the rice pot, Brianna set it on the drain board for Allie to dry. ''Cord's father, Gerald Brannigan, had an affair with my mother that was pretty heated, I gather. But he refused to leave Cord's mother, even after my mother got pregnant with me. I guess he didn't love my mother enough, not that my mother doesn't deserve some of the blame for having the affair in the first place.''

''But you are here now, and Cord calls you sister.''

''When Gerald refused to marry Mother, she moved in with my aunt Elaine in New Hampshire.''

''That is far away?''

''A couple of thousand miles.''

''Ah, that is why you do not speak like the other Texans I have met.''

''My New England accent can still give me away at times.'' Smiling, Brianna labored over the broiling pan, trying to remove bits of meat that had stuck to the surface. ''A few months after I was born, my mother left. Aunt Elaine wasn't at all happy about it, but she kept me and raised me, so I guess I owe her thanks for that.''

Allie sensed Brianna had been made to pay for her mother's sins, a dreadful thing to happen to a child.

''I'd known all along that my father had been married to someone else and lived in Texas, but that's about all I knew until a year or so ago, when my aunt died. Then I found some letters from my mother that my aunt had saved. She'd named my father in them.''

"So you came here."

Brianna drained the water in the sink, which had become too greasy, and started anew. "I called first. I had no idea what kind of reception I'd get from my father. But I was curious. As it happened, Gerald Brannigan died several years ago. And, of course, Cord's mother had left even longer ago than that, when he was pretty young himself."

"She did?" Allie had not thought that Cord might have suffered a loss much like her own, and the revelation touched her heart.

"Given the timing, Gerald's affair might have been part of the problem, but who knows?" Brianna lifted her shoulders as though dismissing the thought. "Anyway, Cord was a little skeptical at first. You know, a total stranger calling up and saying, 'Hi, I'm your long-lost sister.'"

"That would be most startling."

Leaning back, Brianna scanned the room for more pots to scrub. "Cord was really very good about it. He invited me down for a visit, and well…here I am."

Allie wrestled a pot into a low cupboard in a spot where it didn't want to go. Cord's behavior toward his half sister was quite commendable. And surprising. She hadn't imagined beneath his bullying ways he could have a soft heart. The possibility was quite intriguing.

"Unfortunately, any day now I'm going to have to go back to New Hampshire to settle the last details of my aunt's estate—such as it is. I'll have to sign off on the sale of the house where I grew up. I'm not looking forward to the trip."

"Difficult memories can be hard to face."

"It's a way of putting the past behind me." Draining the sink again, Brianna dried her hands on a towel. "That dinner really was delicious, Leila. You know, if you can cook *sarma,* doing tacos and enchiladas would be a cinch."

"I do not even know what an enchilada is."

"How 'bout we do a trade-off? You teach me to make *sarma* and do something creative with eggplant, and I'll teach you how to make American food."

"I do not know that I am good enough to *teach* anything, since I am still learning." And would soon have to return to Munir, she was sure.

"Then we'll learn together. See, the thing is..." Color rose to Brianna's cheeks. "As a kid, I used to dream of some Prince Charming showing up at my door and carrying me off to his castle. If my dream man happens to be an Arab prince, it'd be neat if I could cook him a meal he'd enjoy."

Allie laughed. She could not help herself. "If your Prince Charming is an Arab, you had best hope he is not as arrogant and bossy as Sheikh Rafe."

"That bad, huh?"

"I pity the poor woman who finds herself married to him." Although Rafe could be charming when he chose to be, something he rarely did for Allie's benefit.

"In that case, I'll be sure to pick a different prince. But I'd still love to learn to cook some Arab dishes. Do we have a deal?"

Allie hesitated for only a heartbeat before extending her hand to seal their bargain. "A deal, for however long I am at the Flying Ace. Besides, I have a fantasy, too."

"Oh? What's that?" Brianna's blue eyes sparked with interest.

"I used to imagine a handsome desert sheikh dressed in his flowing robes mounting the wall that surrounds the women's quarters and whisking me away to his secret compound on his mighty steed. Of course, I've outgrown such childish dreams."

Brianna laughed. "Me, too. But without our dreams, life would be pretty dull, wouldn't it?"

Which was why Allie had slipped away from the life she was supposed to lead, if only to provide herself with a few memories after she returned to Munir.

CORD NEEDED SOME ANSWERS.

After another sleepless night—which had nothing to do with indigestion but everything to do with Allie—he saddled Jimmy Boy, his favorite gelding quarter horse, and rode over to the Desert Rose. The Colemans were early risers. Chances were good he'd catch one of the brothers in or around the paddocks at this hour.

The sky was overcast, the air heavy with the threat

of rain. Which was fine by Cord. Summer rains helped keep the grazing good for his cattle, fattening them up for the fall shipment to market.

He found Mac Coleman working a colt on a longe line in the outdoor riding ring. As tall and dark as his twin brother, Cade, Mac had more horse savvy than any man Cord had ever known. He seemed to speak their language. The horses he trained were a pure joy to watch at work.

Dismounting, Cord dropped Jimmy Boy's reins to the ground, knowing he wouldn't move an inch for anything less than a wildfire, and strode over to the ring.

Mac looked up, nodding a greeting. "Hey, Cord, you about ready to turn in that ol' hay burner of yours for a decent horse?"

"I don't know. How 'bout I take one of your fancy all-strut-and-no-work mules out to round up a few head of beef and we'll see how he does?"

Mac laughed at their ongoing joke comparing the relative merits of pure-blooded Arabians with the highly skilled cutting horses a cattleman rode. "Not one of Jabar's offspring, I can tell you that. I've got too big an investment to risk letting an amateur cowboy like you come anywhere near one of his foals."

The truth was, Cord had actually purchased one of the horses from the Coleman stables last year—and had to sell it back. One of the stable hands, Olivia, had raised Prince practically by hand, and he'd matured into a beautiful animal. Needing money, Olivia had sold Prince to Cord. But the following day,

Livy's own personal Prince Sharif Asad Al Farid—Rose Coleman-El Jeved's fourth son—had offered twice the price if Cord would sell Livy's precious horse back to him. Reluctantly, Cord had returned the horse at the same price he'd paid.

He wasn't at all surprised when a few days later Livy and Prince Sharif had announced their forthcoming marriage.

Tilting his hat back, Cord folded his arms across the top railing and watched Mac work the colt. The animal had beautiful lines and a sleek coat, like all of the Desert Rose stock.

Mac brought the colt to a halt. "Something I can do for you?"

"Not really. I was just wondering what you knew about this Sheikh Rafe fellow who was here recently."

"Knows his horseflesh. Nice enough guy, I suppose."

"He seem like a fair man?" One who wouldn't marry his sister off to a wife murderer?

"We shook hands on a business deal. I felt like I could trust him. Why did you want to know?"

"No particular reason," Cord lied. "How about his sister? She was in the States with him, too, wasn't she?"

Idly, Mac stroked the colt's neck. "Yeah, she was here. I didn't see much of her, though, or the woman who came with her. Rafe spent most of his time in the horse barn or paddocks, checking out the stock, and I hung around to answer questions."

"Then you don't know what his sister looks like?"

"Not really. They stayed in town, not here at the ranch. Someone told me the princess was an excellent rider, though." He walked the colt over to the fence. "Cade's wife might have talked with her some. They probably speak the same language. You could ask Rena."

"Naw, that's all right." Cord didn't want to make his curiosity too obvious by asking questions of everyone at the Desert Rose, largely because he didn't know what he'd do with whatever answer he got. "So how are Abbie and the baby?"

Mac beamed, easily distracted by thoughts of his wife and their child. "Beautiful, both of them. Sarah will be walking on her own any day now. She already pulls herself up and stands on her own."

The colt nosed up against the fence, demanding Cord's attention, and he rubbed the animal's velvety muzzle. "Once she starts walking you'll be in *real* trouble."

"Probably. So how's that new housekeeper of yours who you rescued from a near death experience?"

"Fine. And it wasn't that big a deal." He tried to act casual about the whole affair. Although he couldn't feel all that easy about the kiss he and his ersatz housekeeper had almost shared when he soothed her blistered palms following the chicken coop incident. "She cooked *sarma* last night."

"Really? My mother made that a couple of times

while she was here. It's not easy to put together, I gather.''

"Yeah, well…" Cord tugged his hat down firmly on his head. "I gotta go. Say hello to Abbie for me."

"Will do."

As he walked back to Jimmy Boy, Cord could feel Mac's eyes on his back. He'd already asked too many questions. And all he'd learned was that Rafe appeared to be an honest businessman. And Cord still had no proof one way or the other about his housekeeper's identity.

Maybe Nick Grayson, the executive vice president of Coleman-Grayson Investment Company, would know something about Sardar Bin Douri. He had dealings in the oil business. But Nick and his wife, Jessie—Mac's cousin—were still on their honeymoon, and Cord imagined neither one of them would appreciate a phone call from him, even if he knew how to reach them.

Odd how there'd been such a rash of marriages around the Desert Rose in the past year or so. If there was something in the water causing all that matrimony, he hoped whatever it was didn't seep across the property line into his well.

He checked Jimmy Boy's cinch and was about to swing up into the saddle when Mac called to him.

"As I was passing through the kitchen earlier, it smelled like Vi was making cookies. She probably wouldn't mind if you dropped in to say hello."

Remembering all the times he'd raided the Coleman cookie jar as a kid, Cord grinned. "Sounds like a plan to me."

He mounted and reined Jimmy Boy toward the main house. Throughout his adolescent years he'd been envious of the Coleman family, particularly because they had a loving mother in Vi Coleman, who was there for the kids whenever they needed her. Of course, at the time he hadn't known Vi was really the twins' and Alex's aunt, or that their own mother, Rose Coleman-El Jeved Al Farid, had been forced to give her sons to her brother Randy and his wife, Vi, to raise in order to protect their lives.

However unusual the Coleman family background might be, Vi's cookies were one of the best memories of Cord's childhood.

At the back of the house, he dismounted and went up the steps. His knock brought Vi to the door.

Her smile welcomed him as she opened the door. "My sakes, Cord Brannigan! Did you smell my cookies baking clear over to the Flying Ace?"

"Not quite. I got a little hint from Mac down at the riding ring."

"Whatever brings you here, you're always welcome, you know that. Come on in. I just pulled a batch of chocolate chip with walnuts out of the oven."

Taking his hat off, he followed her inside, where the smell of fresh-baked cookies made his stomach growl. Vi Coleman was a good-looking woman in her middle years, her red hair just showing a touch of gray at the temples. She was one of those women who just naturally took to mothering. She'd even been known to keep Cord in line with a gentle word when he'd needed it. And sometimes not so gentle, now that he thought about it.

He picked up a cookie still warm from the oven and tasted it, letting it melt in his mouth. "Vi, I swear you ought to enter these in the county fair."

She laughed. "I'll fix you up a bagful to take home to Brianna."

"She'd like that." So would his housekeeper, Cord imagined.

Unable to resist, he reached for another cookie and noticed a stack of snapshots on the counter. The top one was of Cade and Sheikh Rafe with a pregnant mare. Idly, Cord flipped through the rest of the pictures. He stopped at a candid shot of the sheikh and the woman who was now his housekeeper.

Clearing his throat, he casually asked, "Who's this with the sheikh?"

A spoonful of cookie dough in her hand, Vi glanced over. "That's his sister, Allie. It's not a very good picture, I'm afraid. I've got a new camera and I'm still getting used to it."

Cord slipped the photo back into the pile. The snapshot was good enough for him to know for sure that Allie and his housekeeper were one and the same.

He'd gotten the answer he'd been looking for.

What the photo didn't tell him was *why* a princess would masquerade as a servant. Or how he could get Allie to be honest with him.

A SACK OF COOKIES in his saddlebag, Cord took the long way back home, checking the fence line as he went and pondering those questions.

He found a couple of posts that needed shoring up and took care of it while he was there. He had the herd divided into several sections, making it easier to move them from one pasture to another. He had no idea how the early Texas cowboys had herded hundreds of head of longhorn cattle all the way to a railhead without losing half of them in the process.

Then again, maybe they had, and the old Western movies ignored that little detail.

When he got back to the main ranch, he reined Jimmy Boy to an abrupt halt.

What the hell was Mischief up to now?

From where he sat, it looked like Princess Allie was cleaning a window, precariously perched on a stepladder that was leaning up against the house. Tucked into her tight-fitting jeans, her cute little behind wiggled as she stretched to reach the farthest pane. She was going to break her damn neck!

Dismounting, he worked his way past the low landscaping to where she was working.

"Guess I ought to be glad I don't have a two-story house or you'd really break your neck."

"Oh!" Startled, she tried to whirl around, but got her legs twisted in the ladder rungs in the process and lost her balance. Her arms cartwheeled. She cried out and fell backward into Cord's waiting arms.

She didn't weigh much, but he still staggered under the sudden onslaught. He righted himself and cradled her, his arms around her. She fit nicely right where she was, her almond-shaped eyes wide with surprise, her hand instinctively hooked around the back of his neck. It was all too easy to imagine carrying her inside, to his bedroom.

Which was a thought he didn't dare dwell on, particularly now he knew damn well she was a princess—engaged to marry another man.

"Do you always fall into a man's arms, or is it just my undeniable attraction?"

She drew a shaky breath. "Do you always frighten a woman to death by sneaking up on her?"

"I rode up on a horse. If you'd been paying attention—"

"I was washing windows, as *you* ordered, master. Now, put me down!"

"I'm not your master or anybody else's."

Allie struggled to escape his embrace. It was far too intimate having him hold her, his biceps flexing and his breath fanning her face in a warm caress. His chest felt too rock solid. His eyes were no longer shaded with green and gold, but dark with masculine interest.

Panic, and another feeling she was afraid to name, rushed through her like a desert wind, and her mouth went dry. The more she twisted and turned, brushing her breasts against his broad chest, the worse her riot of emotions became.

He lowered her feet to the ground but didn't entirely release her, continuing to support her. Which was just as well, since her knees felt too wobbly to hold her upright.

"I was almost through with the windows." Her voice sounded thready even to her own ears.

"I'll finish the job for you." His voice sounded gruff. And sexy.

"I have done all of those on the inside of the house." Including those in his spacious bedroom, where she had averted her eyes, if not her thoughts, from the large bed in which he slept.

"You've had a busy day."

"As is appropriate for a housekeeper of such a wealthy and powerful man." His lips quirked into a smile, one that elevated the temperature of her already overheated body. She placed her palms on his chest, felt his heart beating beneath her hand. "If you will please let me go."

His gaze boring into hers, he waited for the longest time before he released her. Immediately she missed his strength surrounding her. His arms holding her. And she knew she should not let that be.

She tossed her head, determined to regain control of her errant thoughts. "Brianna has agreed to teach me to make tacos tonight."

He cocked a brow in apparent surprise. "Great. I'll look forward to dinner."

She fled, leaving Cord to deal with the bucket of soapy water and sponges she'd used to clean the windows. She didn't know what else to do. Being in his arms had been too disconcerting, muddling her brain.

Even as Brianna showed her how simple making tacos was, she had trouble concentrating.

After dinner, she strolled outside, trying to calm her erratic emotions. Near the barn she noticed a mother raccoon with two babies sniffing around for some supper of their own. They were precious creatures, tiny bandits wearing little black masks.

Going back into the house, she gathered a tin plate of fruit and leftover beans, then took it outside to leave for the animals.

Mittens had followed along with her, and started licking at the beans, so Allie scooped the kitten up into her arms.

"You have your own dinner inside," she whispered. "These animals have only what we share with them. Do not be greedy, my sweet."

As she went back into the house, she was pleased with herself. Surely Cord would not deny such innocent creatures a few extra morsels of the food she had helped prepare for his dinner.

It was only the next morning when she woke at dawn to the sound of a frantically bawling calf and Cord's bellow, "Mischief, get your butt out here in a hurry!" that she worried she might have made a serious mistake in judgment.

Chapter Six

She found Cord near the barn, dragging a frightened calf by a rope around his neck. The young animal kicked with his hind legs and tossed his head back and forth, frantic to escape. Terrified by what was happening.

"What is it? What is wrong?" Allie raced across the yard toward Cord.

He ignored her, instead yelling at Ty, who'd come out of the bunkhouse only half-dressed. "Get me some needle-nosed pliers and a bucket!"

"You got it, boss." Racing away, Ty headed into the barn.

"What are you doing to that poor creature?" she demanded. "You're scaring him."

"It's not what I'm doing that's the problem." He maneuvered the calf between two sections of metal fences that formed a chute with only a small gap between them. "It's what a big dose of curiosity and one porcupine can do that's caused this little heifer trouble."

The animal's screams became even more frantic as

Cord pressed the two sides of the metal chute together, allowing only the calf's head to stick out.

"If the problem is curiosity, why did you summon me?"

"Take a look at where the calf stuck his nose."

Confused, Allie glanced around the barnyard, then eyed the calf more closely. She gasped when she realized the poor thing's nose was covered with porcupine quills. "How did such a thing happen?"

Lashing the two sides of the chute together so the calf wouldn't get free, Cord grunted. "*Somebody* left a plate of food out, the porcupine smelled it and helped himself. That's where the calf cornered him."

An uneasy feeling pricked at her conscience. "But I meant the food for the mother raccoon and babies I saw rooting around the chicken coop."

"I guess the porcupine was quicker."

"And the calf got curious?"

"You're catching on, Mischief. Food can draw a lot of critters around here, and turning the Flying Ace into a meal stop for all of them isn't a good plan."

Ty handed Cord the pliers, and by now all the ranch hands had gathered to see what the commotion was about.

It was about Allie doing something foolish, she realized. Her fault that the animal had been injured. A band of regret tightened around her chest.

"I'm sorry," she whispered. "Except for riding horses, I have never been around animals. I didn't know—"

"Yeah, I figured that."

Using the pliers, Cord pulled out a quill and dropped it into the bucket. The calf screamed in pain.

Allie felt sick to her stomach. Helplessly she watched as Cord removed another quill. There had to be a dozen or more of those barbed quills stabbed into the soft tissue of the calf's nose.

Her fault. She'd been so stupid! So thoughtless!

Edging to the other side of the chute, she did the only thing she could think to do. She petted the calf's head, soothing the creature, murmuring soft words.

"It will be over soon, my precious. Cord does not mean to hurt you, but he must remove the quills. You will feel better when they are all gone, I promise you."

As Cord yanked each quill, slowly covering the bottom of a bucket with the evil things, she winced and felt the calf's deep pain in her heart as though she were the one being pierced.

A few drops of rain began to fall, spattering onto the dusty ground and dampening her hair. She paid them no heed, continuing to stroke the animal and croon to it.

Adjusting his grip on the pliers, Cord glanced over at Allie. The tears coursing down her face as she spoke to the calf did something to his heart, easing a tightness that had been there as long as he could remember. Filling an empty spot he'd tried to ignore for most of his life.

She seemed unaware that she was crying, her only concern for the dumb beast who'd stuck her nose where it shouldn't have been. Allie could have been this animal's mother, the way she was soothing the creature. Loving it.

A lump formed in Cord's throat. A senseless reaction at wanting that kind of love and concern for himself.

He was a grown man, for God's sake. He didn't need anyone fawning over him. Certainly not mothering him. He hadn't needed a mother since he'd been twelve years old. He and his dad had gotten along just fine without a woman around the house.

Even so, Cord knew deep in his gut that if Allie ever had a child, she'd never leave him. Never abandon him. No matter how difficult the situation or how hard her life might become. She wouldn't quit. She was too stubborn for that.

Maybe that was something that came with being royalty.

The calf bucked its head, and Cord went back to work, yanking at the embedded quills. But now more than ever he was aware of Allie's soft, lyrical voice, hearing it as though she were talking to him.

"You're being so brave, my sweet. He's almost done. Soon you will be free and able to run. The hurt will be all gone. I promise."

The rain fell harder as a thick, black cloud passed overhead. Raindrops mixed with her tears like diamonds on her cheeks, but Allie didn't budge from her spot beside the calf. Her dark hair hung lank and straight, dripping water. Her cotton blouse soaked through in no time. It took a stubborn woman not to seek shelter in the increasing downpour. Cord had to admire that.

"There, I think I've got them all."

"Thank goodness. You see, my precious, you will be fine now."

Cord rubbed the animal's nose and muzzle to ease the pain, then felt inside the mouth, around the lips and gums for any quills he might have missed.

"Somebody get me that tube of antibiotic ointment," Cord ordered. When no one responded, he looked up. His hired hands had all taken shelter in the barn. Only Allie, mischief maker and princess, had stuck with him.

"If you tell me where it is, I will get what you need," she said.

He needed *her* in ways he hadn't thought possible. To work beside him. To have his children, raise them here on the Flying Ace.

But a princess wasn't raised to get her hands dirty on a working cattle ranch. To wash windows and clean out a chicken coop. That wasn't the life she deserved or had been trained to live. Over time she would learn to hate the man who trapped her into such a harsh life.

He wouldn't be the one to do that to her.

"You'd never be able to find the ointment in the tack room." Shoving his thoughts aside, along with the unexpected image of Allie holding his babies, he waved at his men, shouting that he needed ointment.

Red Galliger broke ranks with the men gawking from the safety of the barn doorway, and vanished

inside. A minute later, he trotted over to the loading
chute where Cord had the calf corraled, handing him
the ointment. When the other men gathered around,
rain dripping from the brims of their Stetsons, Allie
eased away.

Cord wanted to go after her. But his first responsibility was to the injured animal. His father had
taught him well that on the Flying Ace, cattle came
first, before any "dadburn female." Cord wondered
if that had been another reason his mother had left
after she'd learned of his father's affair with Brianna's
mother.

DESPITE THE RAIN, the air was still warm. Sultry. But
that didn't stop the shivers racking Allie as she ran
through the kitchen into her room. She ignored
Brianna, who was seated at the kitchen table.

Allie had done a terrible thing. She didn't belong
on Cord's ranch. In her stupidity, she had caused the
injury of an innocent animal. Her pampered, self-
centered life in an opulent palace with servants to
fulfill her every wish had prepared her poorly for the
realities outside that realm.

She was Cinderella in reverse, her glass slippers
shattered, and she needed to go home.

Except Munir no longer seemed like home.

A sob lodged in her throat as she tore off her wet
blouse and shimmied out of her damp jeans. She
could no longer hide from her brother, from her fate.
She must face her responsibilities, however distasteful
they might be. Surely the rumors of Sardar's wife's

death were false. Servants were notoriously unreliable in relating the truth.

Grabbing a towel from her small bathroom, she scrubbed at her hair, tangling the wet strands.

She would pack, then ask Ty or one of Cord's hired hands to drive her to Austin. From there she would fly home. Staying in a place where she had caused so much trouble was no longer a choice.

But she would always, *always* dream of Texas. And Cord.

CORD SLAPPED HIS STETSON against his thigh and hung it up on the peg by the back door. He needed to talk to Allie. She'd run off too fast. He needed to tell her the calf would be fine and might even remember the lesson she'd learned about sticking her nose in places it didn't belong. Although that was doubtful. Just like people, some cows had a knack for getting into mischief.

He halted when he saw Brianna at the kitchen counter. "You know where Al—Leila is?"

"She blew through here in a hurry a few minutes ago. I saw you had some trouble with a calf out there and decided it would be better if I didn't get in your way."

"Right." He glanced toward Allie's closed bedroom door. "She in there?"

"So far as I know. Last night she said she'd teach me today how to make tabbouleh."

"Tab—who?"

Brianna laughed, the shy giggle she gave sometimes. "It's bulgar wheat with mint flavoring."

"Whatever happened to mashed potatoes and gravy?" he muttered.

"We'll get to that. Give us time."

He wondered if Allie would be here long enough to master the basics of down-home cooking.

He rapped his knuckles on her door.

"Go away," came her voice from inside.

Glancing over his shoulder, he noticed Brianna was making a point to mind her own business. Good for her.

Turning the knob, Cord opened Allie's door, stepped inside, closing it behind him. His timing couldn't have been better—or worse, depending on whose point of view you were talking about. She'd apparently stripped off her wet clothes down to her underwear. Now she snatched up a towel to cover herself, but not before he'd caught a quick glimpse of her delicate breasts, the nipples a dusky shade of rose.

Her eyes wide, she backed up until her legs hit the bed. "Do American men always enter a woman's bedchamber uninvited?"

"Only when they're concerned about the woman." He glanced around the room, at the open closet door, the bed piled high with clothes. Her satchel open on the chair. "What's going on here?"

"I'm going back to Munir."

Her announcement knocked the air right out of his lungs. He'd known she'd leave eventually. But not

yet. He wasn't ready to lose her. Panic and dismay
flared in his gut like a bad case of indigestion.

"What brought on this sudden decision?"

"The calf, of course. Because of my stupidity, the
poor creature suffered great pain."

"She's well on her way to recovery."

"That does not excuse my mistake."

"Anyone can make a mistake. You've never lived
on a ranch before."

"No, I have not. Nor have I cooked or cleaned a
chicken coop or washed windows. All of which I have
done very poorly."

"You've had lots of new experiences, but you've
handled them pretty darn well, all things considered."
Particularly the hard time he'd been giving her. Forcing her into a role for which she was ill-equipped.

She blinked. Her damp hair was in disarray, her
chocolate-brown eyes wary as though she didn't believe him. "I have?"

Desperate to find a way to get her to stay, if only
for a few more days, Cord edged closer. "I didn't
think you were a quitter."

"I'm not." She lifted her chin. "But I do not belong here."

"You promised Brianna you'd teach her how to
make, uh, tab-something."

"Tabbouleh."

"So you're going to break your promise, just duck
out on Brianna when she was counting on you? Because things got a little rough out there, huh?"

Allie loosened her grip on the towel and paled. "I could leave her the recipe."

"That wouldn't be the same, would it?" His mouth dry, his jeans growing tighter by the minute, he willed the towel to slip a little lower. A few inches was all he was asking. "Then there's the unfinished windows you're going to leave me to deal with."

"I finished—"

"With the rain coming down as hard as it is, the outsides are going to be a mess when the storm passes. I figured I could help you next time around."

Her mouth formed a silent *O* as he moved closer.

He palmed her cheek, and with his fingers he combed her tangled hair behind her ear. "I've been thinking how hard you've been working and how you needed a break. I thought you'd like to come with me to the stock auction in Austin tomorrow." Impulsively, he'd extended an invitation he hadn't been considering ten minutes ago. "But if you're determined to leave..."

"You are not angry with me about the calf?"

"No." Anger was far from the emotion he was experiencing, although he was reluctant to label his feelings beyond a heavy dose of lust.

"My brother would have been furious with me for doing such a foolish thing."

"I'm not your brother." To prove his point, he leaned forward and kissed her. Her lips were amazingly soft, like rose petals moistened by a morning rain shower, and she sighed into his mouth.

Still palming her face, he slid his thumb back and

forth across her warm, velvety cheek. The temptation to tug the towel from her grasp, to cup and test the texture of her small, round breasts with his hands, was nearly overwhelming.

But he was acutely aware of Brianna only paces away beyond the door. He wouldn't stop at a few caresses, he knew, and his sister would be a near witness to his taking from Allie what wasn't rightfully his to claim. He couldn't embarrass Allie in that way. Or put his sister in such an awkward position.

With more willpower than he'd thought he possessed, he lifted his head and lowered his hand to Allie's shoulder, letting his fingertips drift down her arm, stopping to trace tiny circles above her elbow.

She shuddered and slowly opened her eyes. Her pupils were dilated, her eyelids heavy with desire. He called himself all kinds of a fool for not taking advantage of her willingness. For not taking her fully in his arms, laying her on the cluttered bed and easing the painful ache that had formed between his legs.

His throat was thick with need as he spoke. "So do you think you might want to stick around for a while?"

The tip of her tongue peeked out to sweep across her lips, making them glisten. "It would not be kind of me to break my promise to Brianna."

"And a trip to Austin? Just for the day?"

"Would be most interesting."

"I'm sure it will be. We'll leave early in the morning."

Her gaze held his, a plea in her eyes along with a question. "I'll be ready whenever you are."

He wasn't sure she realized what she had said or what she was agreeing to be ready for. He only knew he had to get out of her room while there was still time. Before his libido overruled his brain, which was what would happen if he stayed here a moment longer.

Allie gaped at Cord as he backed away, jerked open the door and bolted toward the kitchen, swinging the door shut behind him. The shivers that had assailed her earlier returned in the form of gooseflesh racing down her spine. Her knees turned watery, and she sank heavily onto the edge of the bed.

Cord had kissed her.

The first man ever to do so, and his flavor was still on her lips—spicy and fresh. Tempting and deliciously masculine. She'd been sure her heart would fly out of her chest, it had beat so wildly. Even now she could barely draw a steady breath.

He had kissed her, then run from the room.

Had she done something wrong? Granted, she was as lacking in experience in the art of kissing as she was at cooking. But she was learning. He should have at least given her a second chance if she had failed the first time. Fairness demanded her whole life not be determined by a single incident where she had faltered for lack of training.

Stunned by her apparent inadequacy, she grabbed up the first pair of dry jeans she found, pulled them on, along with her boots and a blouse. She would have to find some way to get Cord to kiss her again. The next time, she vowed, he wouldn't run away so quickly.

On the service porch, she found a yellow rain slicker, which she tugged on. It rained so seldom in Munir that it was a treat for her to splash through the downpour to the chicken coop to collect the morning supply of eggs.

The rooster's harem of hens were huddled on their nests. The rooster came out to greet her, crowing loudly.

"I know your feathers do not like rain." She gave one of the hens a tentative shove to get her off the nest so she could check for an egg. "But rain makes the grass and trees grow and the grain that you and your women eat. So rain is good, yes?"

He clucked, bobbing his head up and down in agreement.

"I don't suppose you can provide me with advice about how a woman can get a man to kiss her again."

Scratching the ground, he pecked at an invisible piece of grain, ignoring her question. Just like a man.

Allie plucked an egg from the next nest and put it in the basket she carried. "No," she sighed. "I did not think that you would be of any help." Romance was never a problem for men. They simply strutted and clucked, making women fall at their feet.

She gathered the rest of the eggs without the hens doing her any damage, and took them back to the house. The rain had let up to a light drizzle. Above the trees to the south a small patch of blue shone through the clouds. Tomorrow would be clear, she thought.

Perhaps it would be better to consult with a woman on matters such as kissing.

A RAINY DAY WAS a good time to work on the tack. And the tack room was a good place for a man to hide out and get his thoughts together.

Hefting his best show saddle, Cord carried it to a stand where he could clean it.

When Sandra had dumped him for a married man, he'd reached a couple of decisions. He was going to lay off women altogether, and if he was tempted to do otherwise, he sure as hell wasn't going to get involved with a woman who was committed to another man.

He hadn't planned on Allie showing up in his life, creating mischief and getting under his skin.

Pouring a little ammonia into a pail of water, he used a sponge to get rid of the dirt and grime on the saddle, working around the silver ornamentation and the Western designs cut into the rich leather.

If only Allie would be up front with him about who she was. That would help him figure out where he stood. He didn't want to be a pawn in some game the princess was playing, and then have her trot on back to Munir, happy as a clam to marry some other guy. Sandra had been a helluva good actress. Maybe Allie was, too—a pampered princess wanting to sow a few wild oats with a Texas cowboy, earning herself a notch on her royal bedpost.

He couldn't even be sure her story about the man she was to marry—a man she suspected murdered his first wife—was true. No matter what kind of politics was involved, it didn't seem possible the sheikh would put his own sister at risk.

The rain had let up, leaving only the sound of a steady drip coming off the barn roof. Inside, the smell of ammonia mixed with the scent of hay and damp earth, but it wasn't enough to clear Cord's mind.

Maybe he ought to go along with Allie's game until she either told him the truth or took off. He knew the score. If he kept his emotions out of the mix, it was no big deal. He could play wait-and-see.

But this time he'd make damn sure he wasn't the one who got hurt. He'd made a fool of himself once by falling in love with the wrong woman. He wasn't going to do it again, sure as hell not with a princess who was a royal pain—and just happened to twist his libido into a knot by simply walking into the room.

THAT AFTERNOON, while making tabbouleh, Allie watched Brianna chopping fresh mint on the cutting board, and bolstered her courage to ask the question she had been pondering since morning.

"How do you get a man to kiss you?"

Brianna's head jerked up. She let out a sharp cry before her hand flew to her mouth and she sucked her finger.

"Did you hurt yourself?" Allie asked.

"I practically cut off my finger!" Brianna gasped. "Where on earth did that question come from?"

Heat rose to Allie's cheeks as quickly as the summer sun scorched the desert.

"Now that was a dumb question, wasn't it?" Brianna's blue eyes twinkled. "Cord?"

Impossibly, Allie's embarrassment deepened and her whole body flushed. "I should not have spoken of such things to his sister. I am sorry—"

"Don't be, please." Brianna rinsed her finger under running water, then wrapped a paper towel around the cut, which wasn't as bad as Allie had feared. "I'm just not sure I'll be much help when it comes to a woman attracting a man and getting him to kiss her."

"But you are an American. Surely you know what American men like when they kiss a woman."

"Oh, Leila..." Brianna's shy giggle was accompanied by a flush to her own cheeks. "I have about enough experience with men to fill a thimble."

"That is not a great deal, is it?"

"If you rely on my advice, it will be like the blind leading the blind."

Allie had not expected that. She had assumed a woman raised in America, with all the freedom and independence permitted here, would know a great deal more about men than she did. Hollywood movies certainly depicted American women that way. Apparently, in Brianna's case, that was not true.

Exhaling slowly, Allie concluded she would have to rely on her own instincts and hope for the best.

Chapter Seven

"This is a very nice truck."

"Like most ranch vehicles, it takes a beating. But she still runs good."

Sitting next to Cord in the cab of the pickup, Allie considered the biggest drawback was the shifting mechanism on the floor, which kept her from sitting close to him. How, she wondered, could she encourage a second kiss if she was forced to remain at arm's length? The limousines in which she usually rode would not create this sort of a problem.

They'd risen before dawn to leave for the stock auction in Austin. Now, driving into the rising sun, Cord was wearing dark glasses, which made him look daring, as though he were the leader of a desert caravan heading off into uncharted lands. Except the landscape lacked sand dunes and there wasn't a camel in sight.

She watched him shift gears with ease as he slowed to round a turn on the highway, then accelerate again.

"Why is the shifter not on the console like other cars?"

"It's a five-speed, and the truck's a three-quarter ton. We do a lot of hauling hay and animals, like in the trailer we're pulling now. On a working ranch we need lower gears and more torque than a passenger car has." Behind them, the empty animal trailer had the Flying Ace logo on the sides in the shape of a playing card with wings.

"I have only driven cars with automatic transmissions." Rarely had she been allowed to drive any vehicle in Munir, since servants drove her wherever she needed to go. But twice she had convinced her chauffeur to allow her to drive in unpopulated areas—with mixed results. The damage she had done to the black Mercedes had not been severe, in her view. Her brother had disagreed. "Perhaps you will teach me to drive this truck someday?"

Cord slanted her a glance, although she couldn't see his eyes through his tinted glasses. "You'll be better off to stick with a four-speed automatic. You'll get yourself into less trouble that way."

She sniffed. He had so little faith in her ability. Perhaps a time would come when she could prove him wrong.

As they grew closer to Austin, the traffic on the highway increased and so did Allie's excitement. Shopping, in its myriad forms, always provided her a pleasant diversion—even if the shopping was for large animals.

"Tell me about this auction we are going to."

"I'm hoping to buy a two-year-old bull with a mid-rating on weight gain."

She looked at him blankly. "You do not already have bulls in your herd?"

"Sure I do, four of them. They're my backup, covering the ladies and doing the job if artificial insemination doesn't take. But Bart's getting on in years. Not as fertile as he used to be."

"So you wish to buy a bull in his prime."

"You got it."

"Just as you are a man in your prime, able to make strong, healthy babies."

Coughing, he jerked the wheel, taking the truck out of its lane, and he had to wrestle the vehicle back into line. He cleared his throat twice before he could speak.

"I don't usually think of myself in quite those terms."

"Why not?" Allie certainly did, although she hadn't given the topic a great deal of thought until now. Cord would provide a woman with robust, vigorous babies, which was what she assumed he'd want in a bull. "Men of your age must be at their best, reproductively speaking. Your conformation is excellent—broad shoulders, long, muscular legs, intelligence. At auction you would no doubt draw a high bid. Surely a bull is judged in the same way. Camels are."

He sputtered, again nearly running them off the road into the ditch. Beads of sweat appeared on his forehead. "Maybe we could change the subject before I get us both killed, okay?"

Allie smiled to herself. She had no idea a man as

experienced as Cord would have such difficulty discussing the elements he would look for in a breeding animal. Such a topic frequently arose in the women's quarters when they were comparing men.

Cord would do well in their ratings.

HUNDREDS OF TRUCKS with trailers jammed the parking lot at the stock show. Cowboys strutted around in boots and Stetsons, their faces weathered, their legs bowed. Cattle of every size and color, from almost pure white to midnight-black, plus mixed shades in between, snorted and stomped in fenced-off pens, stirring up a cloud of dust that coated Allie's clothes and clogged her throat. The bazaar in Munir had never been this hectic.

Cord's hand placed lightly at the small of her back was reassuring as he ushered her through the maze of aisles past the penned animals.

"That's a magnificent bull." Allie made it a point not to step near the huge animal, its coat a lighter shade of tan than most. "Your cows would appreciate him?"

"Probably not. He's too big. I've got a mixed herd of Herefords and shorthorns. That's an American Brahma, a terrific specimen, I agree. But if he covered one of my smaller cows, he'd hurt her."

"Oh, dear. We would not want that."

His lips twitched with the hint of a smile and his eyes twinkled with mirth. "It helps if the bull and his cows are pretty much a match in size for each other."

Allie recognized Cord was taller than six feet and

she was no more than five feet five inches tall. Did he think they were not a match? Was that why he had so abruptly halted their kiss?

Lowering her voice to what she hoped was a seductive whisper, she said, "I am sure a woman who is interested enough could accommodate a man of any size."

He coughed and thumped his chest with his fist, trying to draw a breath.

"Are you coming down with a cold?"

He looked at her with tears filling his eyes. Pulling a white handkerchief from his pocket, he wiped his eyes, then resettled his beige Stetson on his head.

"I'm fine, Mischief. Just be careful what you say. This is a public place."

She huffed, pretending not to know what he was talking about. She was simply trying to express an interest in his cattle breeding program, or so she wanted him to think. In fact, she thought she and Cord would match quite nicely. At least his kiss had led her to believe that was so. The shape of his lips had fit perfectly with hers. His hand on her cheek had both soothed and aroused. Surely that was a good beginning, one that she wanted to pursue further.

They came to another bull that seemed particularly agitated, swinging his head back and forth, digging his hoof into the ground.

"Now that's a wild-eyed ridge runner if I ever saw one," Cord commented. "He'd scare the bejeebers out of my cows. They wouldn't let him get anywhere near them."

Allie tended to agree. Despite magnificent shoulders and a muscular body, there was madness in the animal's eyes. She'd never go near a creature like that, either.

Another bull Cord judged to be post-legged. "He wouldn't be able to mount a cow easily. He'd wear himself out."

"I should not think you would have such a difficulty."

He shot her a startled look, and when she smiled, he rolled his eyes. "I should have left you at the ranch."

"But then you would not be enjoying yourself so much."

He looped his arm around her shoulders. "You're determined to drive me crazy, aren't you, Mischief?"

"If you say so, master," she teased. Eager to be as close to Cord as she could, she slid her arm around his waist.

Stopping by a food stand, Cord bought hot dogs drenched in chili—a down-home Texas dish, he told her—and standing at tiny round tables, they sipped beer while eating the messy concoction for lunch. The spices zinged through her, but with no less fire than the heat building within her because of Cord. She imagined if their lips touched now in a kiss, they would turn the entire stock show into a bonfire.

When they finished eating, they continued walking through the maze, Allie acutely aware of the brush of his thigh against hers, the weight of his arm around her. Wherever their bodies met, heat radiated like a desert sun, burning her with a secret desire she knew was forbidden. The man to whom she was betrothed would demand a virgin.

Still, she'd heard talk of ways to fake that virginal state if a woman wanted to seek her pleasure before the marital bed. She wished now that she had paid closer attention to that conversation. Surely if such a situation came to pass, her ladies-in-waiting would be able to provide the answers she would need.

Losing her virginity would therefore not create an undue problem, *if* the opportunity presented itself, she thought with a delighted grin.

A short, stout man approached them, extending his hand to Cord. "Howdy, young man. Haven't seen you in half an age."

Cord's smile broadened as he took the man's hand. "Samuel, good to see you. Heard your boy got his Ph.D. in aeronautics. Congratulations."

"Yep. Can't keep 'em down on the farm these days. Too many other choices." He sent a pointed look in Allie's direction. "Looks like you're doing mighty fine."

"Yes, uh, this is Leila Khautori. Meet Samuel Lester from out Johnson City way." Cord slid his arm around Allie's waist again. "She's, uh, staying at the Flying Ace for a while."

"Well, now, the missus will be mighty interested to hear that. She always said sooner or later you'd find yourself the purdiest woman in the state."

"I'm his housekeeper," Allie said, not sure whose

reputation she was determined to protect—hers or Cord's.

"Yes, ma'am, that's mighty fine—you and him, I mean. Cord here's about as good an ol' boy as you'll find in these parts. Sold me a yearling bull a few years back that just couldn't seem to do his job. Cord did the right thing. Took him back and gave me a full refund, no questions asked."

"The least I could do," Cord conceded. "You lost a whole season."

"No way you could've told that ahead of time, though. Not every man would've done what you did. Makes a man proud to call you friend."

The two men shook hands again, Cord looking a little embarrassed by the exchange. In contrast, Allie's chest filled with pride that Cord was such an honest businessman, willing to take back an animal that hadn't performed well. From the rumors she had heard, Sardar Bin Douri was not so scrupulous in his business dealings.

"Sorry about Samuel jumping to conclusions about us," Cord said. "I could have worked a little harder to explain the situation, but once he gets his head set on something—"

"There is no need to explain anything." At least, not yet. One kiss did not constitute an act for which she or Cord should feel any shame.

He nodded in agreement, a little too vigorously, in Allie's view.

"The bull auction is about to start. How 'bout we make our way to the stands? They'll begin parading the bulls pretty soon, and I want to get a good look before I buy.''

Every man at the auction had his eye on Allie. She stood out like a sparkling diamond among ordinary pebbles. If nothing else, her impractical white Stetson drew attention like a red flag enticed a crazed bull.

Wearing tight-fitting jeans, a tank top that clung to her curves, and high-heeled boots that made her legs look like they went on forever, she was the sexiest woman for miles around. It made Cord proud she was with him—and damn jealous that every man in the stadium was looking at her, wanting her. That wasn't an emotion he experienced often. Hardly ever, that he could recall.

But she brought out his protective instincts. Possessive ones, too. Which was unfortunate, since there was no way she'd remain at the Flying Ace much longer. She'd been there a week. Cord hadn't expected her to last that long.

And she'd already threatened to leave once. Sooner rather than later she'd pack up and be gone. There wasn't any way a Texas rancher with dirt under his fingernails and grime on his skin could keep a princess around for long. It wasn't in the cards.

Unless he found a way to come aces high like his great-grandpa had.

Once burned, he didn't think he'd get the deal he wanted this time, either. Allie was engaged to marry another man.

The first few animals put up for auction were bull calves. Cord, like most of the other bidders sitting in the stands, was looking for a mature bull. The auctioneer used the young animals to warm up the audience, setting the tone for the higher bids that would come later.

"Do you know which bull you will bid on?" Allie asked.

"I've spotted a couple that look good to me." He tapped the program listing the day's offerings. "We'll see how they do when they're brought out to walk around the ring."

Hooking her arm through his, Allie leaned over to read the descriptions of the bulls he'd checked. Despite the dust and animal smells, her sultry scent of jasmine teased at his senses. Feminine. Alluring. When she shifted her head, tossing her long hair back behind her shoulder, Cord's concentration on the auction faltered. The auctioneer's rapid-fire chatter faded into background noise, and all Cord wanted to do was take Allie someplace where they could be alone.

When the first bull he was considering paraded by, Cord forced his thoughts back to business. He jumped in on the third round of bidding, but the price rose so quickly, he decided to let it go.

"You do not want this animal?" Allie asked.

"Too expensive. The high bidders ran up the price too fast. With any luck, they'll run out of steam and cash by the time the next one I'm looking at goes on the auction block."

Fortunately, his prediction was right. He outbid his competitors for bull 164, getting him for a reasonable price.

Standing, he pulled Allie to her feet. "That's it. I've got to pay the cashier and get the bull loaded in the trailer. Then we can be on our way back to the ranch."

Allie linked her fingers though his, disappointed that their outing together was nearly over. In Munir, she rarely had an opportunity to mix with commoners, and the sights and sounds were fascinating. Of course, being anywhere with Cord would be exciting.

He paid for the bull, and they returned to the truck. Dozens of vehicles were jockeying for position, backing trailers up to loading chutes. Cowboys working for the auction company prodded bulls into the chutes for the new owners.

Cord expertly maneuvered the trailer into position. "You wait here," he said as he got out of the truck. "I don't want you trampled in all the confusion."

That was fine with Allie. She had a good view of both the cattle pens and the activity all around them. It looked like a poorly choreographed dance, with cowboys and trucks dodging each other, bulls waiting in the wings for their brief moment on stage—to which some of them made noisy objections. The most obstinate fought entering the chutes and balked again before being prodded into a trailer.

Allie could understand their consternation. She, too, hated to be forced to do things she didn't want to do.

The truck bounced as Cord's bull was loaded into the trailer with a minimum of argument. The handsome bull was apparently sweet tempered as well as a fine specimen.

As she waited for Cord, another man approached the truck. He tipped the brim of his hat.

"Hey, lady, can you move your rig? They've got my bull in the chute ready to go."

"Cord should be back—"

"Just pull her up there, far enough so's I can get my rig in behind yours."

She looked around, desperately trying to spot Cord. "I don't know how—"

"Look, sweetheart, I've got a sick kid in my truck who's likely to puke all over the place if I don't get him home soon. Can you just pull her up a ways?"

"Oh, dear." She vacillated, trying to decide what to do, concerned about the child's well-being versus her lack of driving experience.

Cord had left the key in the ignition. She'd watched him shift on the way into town. Surely it wasn't too difficult to drive a truck, even with the shifter on the floor. She'd seen other women doing it. In America such a thing was common.

Awkwardly hooking her legs over the gearshift, she slid to the driver's side.

"Thanks, lady. Pull her up thataway. Twenty feet or so oughta do her." Tipping his hat again, the cowboy backed away from the cab toward his own truck, which was parked in the lane.

Imitating Cord's actions, she jammed in the left pedal and twisted the key in the ignition. The truck came to life with a gratifying roar. She smiled to herself, pleased to have the opportunity to prove to Cord she wasn't utterly incompetent.

Gently, she eased up with her left foot. The truck lurched forward and the engine died. Behind her, the trailer rocked up and down.

She smiled sheepishly at the waiting cowboy.

"Remember to step on the gas, sweetheart," he shouted.

Ah, so that was what she had done wrong.

Eager to try again, she repeated the earlier process, but this time she gunned the engine before releasing her left foot.

The truck shot forward like a rocket—precisely at the moment a third truck was passing in front of her.

Her foot still on the throttle, Allie yanked the wheel hard to the right. She careened past the oncoming truck, congratulating herself for missing it by mere inches, only to find herself about to run over another cowboy.

She slammed on the brakes and felt the trailer fishtailing behind her. The cowboy dived to safety. The bull in the trailer bellowed a bloodcurdling sound. And the truck staggered to a stop, the engine backfiring, then dying.

An instant later, someone yelled, "Bull on the loose!"

THE MOMENT CORD HEARD the warning shout, he knew Mischief was in trouble again. He never should have left her alone.

Without a word to the guy from a neighboring

ranch who he'd been talking to, he raced toward the spot where he'd left his truck. Of course it wasn't there. Twenty feet away his trailer stood empty, the back gate wide open. He caught a glimpse of his newly purchased bull hightailing it through the parking lot, scattering cowboys as he went.

Cord swore loudly and succinctly. "Somebody get a rope!"

Chapter Eight

An hour later, Allie sat primly on her side of the truck, her hands folded neatly in her lap, intangible waves of anger and frustration washing over her from Cord's side of the pickup. Dirt and sweat streaked his face. There was a rip in his shirt, and his jeans were covered in mud.

She exhaled. So much for her plan to get him to kiss her again.

"I am sorry your bull escaped the trailer, but I was concerned about a sick child. The cowboy said—"

"We would have all been better off if you'd been concerned about the fact you don't know how to drive five-on-the-floor." To emphasize the point, he shifted down to accelerate around a slow-moving car.

"It doesn't look that hard." She pouted, thinking he didn't have to be quite so angry with her. Her intentions had been good. They always were, which was why it was so discouraging that more times than not her best efforts got her into trouble.

"The fact is, Mischief, you don't *think* before you

do anything. You just act. You could have gotten someone killed, or at least seriously injured.''

''No one suffered injury,'' she protested. If she excluded his scraped shoulder, which she probably shouldn't.

''Maybe not, but your little stunt cost me a few hundred bucks I hadn't planned to spend. That bull back there in the trailer did a helluva lot of damage to a few fenders after we had him cornered.''

''I'll pay you back.''

''Right. I'll take it out of your wages.''

She had momentarily forgotten Cord didn't know she was wealthy in her own right. ''Fine. I agree to your terms. I do not wish to be in debt to you.''

''Great. And don't forget to add in the prize bull I just bought is so worn out, he won't be able to mount a cow for months.''

''Then you bought the wrong bull. Any male worth his salt could recover from a vigorous workout more quickly than that.''

His lips quivered with the hint of a grin. ''Mischief, what am I going to do with you? One minute I want to throttle you and the next I...'' Shaking his head, he left the thought unsaid.

''Yes? What is it you might wish to do with me?''

To her disappointment, he waved off her question. ''For now, let's just concentrate on getting us and the bull home in one piece.''

AT THE DESERT ROSE, Cade loaded his three-month-old twins into their car seats in the back of his extended-cab pickup, then helped his wife into the passenger seat.

"Tell me again why you want us to visit Cord's ranch?" Rena asked.

"For one thing, you've barely been out of the house in the past three months. I figured a little outing wouldn't hurt you or the babies."

"That's true enough, but that surely is not the only reason we are going to visit Cord."

"Well, no." His wife was too perceptive by far, he thought as he went around to the driver's side. "Cord's got this new housekeeper, one of Princess Aliah Bahram's ladies-in-waiting. You remember, Cord saved her bacon when her horse ran away with her."

"I recall the story."

"So, I figure she's from Munir, which is close to where you come from. She might be homesick by now."

She glanced at him, frowning. "Is she very beautiful?"

Cade choked, then smoothed her dark auburn hair back behind her ear. "Honey, trust me, you don't have a thing to worry about."

"It has been a long while since—"

"I'll wait, sweetheart, as long as I have to. There's no way on earth I'll risk hurting you."

A sultry smile lifted her lips. "When I visited the doctor this morning, she said I was able to resume my wifely duties whenever I felt like it."

Cade nearly canceled the trip then and there. But

he really needed Rena to check out the woman who had settled herself into Cord's household as a servant. He didn't like the thought of Cord becoming embroiled in the cutthroat world of royal politics.

Tonight, he vowed, would be soon enough for more entertaining activities—assuming Zach and Natalie allowed him a few hours of peace and quiet to get reacquainted with his wife.

THE SUN WAS LOW on the horizon as Cord approached the ranch house. He spotted a Desert Rose truck parked near the house, and he nearly groaned aloud.

He wasn't in the mood for company. He had bruises on his bruises. His shoulder ached from having taken a header trying to lasso that damn bull, and his knee was throbbing for the same reason. He was hot and tired and smelled like he'd been rolling around in manure, which he had.

Worse, he didn't know what to do about Allie.

With the best of motives, she had a knack of making a mess of things. He ought to be packing her off to the airport; he should have done that days ago. Instead, he found himself grinning like a fool half the time, wondering what crazy stunt she'd pull next. He couldn't fault her for caring about a sick kid—or a hungry raccoon, for that matter. But whatever she touched turned out to be like Sherman marching through Georgia. A disaster.

Yet behind the haughty lift of her chin and her imperious ways, he saw a vulnerable woman. One who wanted to please others. To be accepted.

To be loved.

Now there was the rub, he thought as he pulled the truck to a stop. If he allowed himself to love her, what would it get him?

Nothing but more trouble.

A man would be blind stupid to set himself up to cross thousands of years of tradition in a foreign country where arranged marriages were the norm. Hell, Cord would probably have the State Department crawling all over the Flying Ace if he messed with Princess Aliah Bahram. Not that he wasn't tempted.

To his surprise, his visitors were Cade and his wife, Rena, along with their baby twins. Brianna already had one of the infants in her arms; Cade was holding the other one.

Cade sauntered toward the trailer and peered inside as Cord got out of the truck.

"New bull?"

"Yep. Paid a pretty penny for him, too." Plus a few additional charges, courtesy of Allie and her self-taught driving lesson.

Allie hopped down from the truck, making a bee-line for Cade and the infant he was carrying. "Oh, what a beautiful baby," she crooned, caressing the infant's cheek with a single finger. "May I hold her?"

"This one's a him—Zach."

"Boy or girl does not matter. He is such a precious little one." Taking the baby, Allie rocked it in her arms, cooing sweet sounds in a language only an infant would understand.

Cord felt a stab of yearning, picturing Allie as the mother she was meant to be. Holding *his* child. Loving *him*. The image made his knees go weak, as though he'd lasted a full eight seconds in a bronc ride and couldn't catch his breath.

He tried to shake off the feeling, but it lingered in the air like Allie's jasmine perfume, luring him in a direction he didn't want to go.

Brianna strolled up to the truck with a twin in her arms, Rena right behind her, keeping an eye on her babies.

"Aren't the twins adorable, Cord?" Brianna said. "They're three months old now."

He blinked, dragging himself back to some sense of reality. "Yeah. Cute." Instead of the hint of red in the babies' spiky hair, he imagined he saw Allie's shade of pecan-brown.

Cade said, "Rena and I thought Leila might be getting homesick to talk to someone from her part of the world, so we dropped by for a visit."

Allie reacted as though she'd been struck by lightning. Her back went rigid. Her gaze flew to Rena, and recognition flared before she ducked her head, practically shoving Zach back into his father's arms.

"Excuse me, please. I must prepare dinner." She raced off toward the house without a backward glance.

"Did I say something wrong?" Cade asked.

"No, I don't think so." Although Cord suspected he knew the reason Allie had fled so quickly. She didn't want to risk being unmasked, and Rena would be the one person in the county who could do that. Might be Rena's appearance would be the best thing that could happen, prompting Allie to trust Cord and explain why she was masquerading as a servant. "Truth is, this isn't a real good time. I've gotta get this bull up to the north pasture and let him settle in. He's had kind of a hard day."

"Sure, I understand." Cade glanced at his wife, and got a sappy expression on his face. "Fact is, Rena and I sort of have plans for this evening, anyway. The chance came up, uh, unexpectedly."

A flush colored Rena's cheeks, and she took baby Natalie back from Brianna. "We will come visit another time, Cord, and you and your sister must come by our house when you can. You will be most welcome. Your, uh, servant as well."

"Now that I've had a good look at your twins," Brianna said, "I may come by often to get my cuddling fix."

"An extra pair of arms are always welcome."

Back in the truck heading toward the Desert Rose, Cade said, "Leila sure took off in a hurry when we showed up. What do you think?"

"I think she is not Leila at all, but Princess Aliah."

He slowed the truck. "You sure?"

"I only visited with the princess and her brother briefly while they were here. But yes, I am sure."

"I'd better tell Cord, huh? If the princess is hiding out or trying to pull some sort of a scam, he ought to know."

Rena rested her hand on his thigh. "Did you not

see how your friend looked at the princess while she was holding the baby?''

"He looked the same as always. A little tired, maybe, and dirty—"

She laughed, the lyrical sound he loved so much. "Men are so unobservant. Your friend Cord is in love with Princess Aliah."

"Well, shoot, I'd better tell him right away. She's supposed to be engaged to some guy back in Munir. I have the feeling Cord's already been hurt once by some—"

"Hush, my husband. In matters of the heart, some women prefer to select their own mates rather than accept an arranged marriage. I am sure Cord and the princess will be able to work out their own destiny without our interference."

Cade braked the truck to a stop, slipped the gear into Neutral and tugged Rena toward him for a kiss. Rena had been pledged to marry his brother Mac— until Cade went to Balahar in Mac's place. Once he'd met Rena, he'd known he would never give her up to Mac or any other man. Fortunately, Rena had been equally happy with the new arrangement.

Lifting his head, he looked into her beautiful green eyes and smiled. "In matters of the heart, my love, I'll defer to your woman's intuition. And now, since the kids have dozed off, let's get on home...."

IN HER ROOM, Allie curled up on her bed, holding Mittens in her lap. She stroked the kitten's soft fur, listened to her purr and let tears of confusion and fear spill down her cheeks.

She had been at the Flying Ace for a week. She could almost feel the moment of truth coming closer, that time when Rafe would realize she had not returned to Munir with him. And now Princess Serena, Cade's wife, had discovered her presence. Surely she or Cade would tell Cord of her masquerade.

Then she would have to go home.

An ache filled her chest. No doubt Cord would be happy to have her gone, no longer creating mischief for him.

Mischief.

Her watery smile caused another tear to drop onto the top of Mittens's head. She'd never had a nickname before, not like Mischief, and sometimes when Cord spoke the name it was almost like an endearment. When he wasn't righteously angry at her, that is.

She had done a foolish thing today by trying to move the truck. She didn't have much time to make amends for her behavior before, one way or another, he would learn her true identity and she would be forced to return to Munir.

She sighed. What in the name of Constantine could she do that wouldn't create a mess worse than the mistakes she had already made?

That evening, Cord didn't return to the house until late. Brianna had left him a plate of roast beef and potatoes on the stove to reheat if he was hungry. And when Allie arose the next morning, he had already left to help move part of the herd from one pasture to another.

Discouraged, Allie lingered over a cold cup of coffee while Brianna helped herself to a second piece of toast. At her feet, Mittens was attacking her toes with her tiny teeth.

"What would be something nice I could do for Cord?" Allie asked his sister.

Brianna spread a teaspoon of apricot jam on her toast. "Nice? I haven't the vaguest idea. He's so wrapped up in the ranch and keeps everything pretty close to the chest...." She tilted her head, studying Allie. "Is something happening between the two of you I should know about?"

"No, no." Her denial came a little too quickly, although one kiss was hardly worth noting. "I just thought, well, I seem to create so much trouble for him that maybe I could do something he would appreciate. A special favor, perhaps?"

"I really can't think of a thing, but I know what you could do for me, if you're interested."

Given the circumstances, aiding Cord's sister might be the best she could do. "I would be happy to help you, if I can."

"That would be terrific. I have to go into Austin today to see the accountant with my monthly reports, and one of things I'm going to do is buy a new filing cabinet. Everything Cord has is jammed full of stuff and terribly disorganized."

"I do not know that I would be good at filing."

"What I need is some basic sorting. Getting rid of

papers that are more than seven years old, old catalogs, out-dated bank statements. That sort of thing.''

Allie instantly saw a disaster in the making. She was bound to throw away something valuable, like the deed to the ranch. "I couldn't. If I discarded something I shouldn't, Cord would dress me in red and put me in the pasture with the bull he bought yesterday." A fitting end to her week-long adventure.

Brianna laughed. "Oh, don't worry about Cord. I'll get you some boxes. Whatever you find you think can be discarded, you put in the box, and I'll take a look at it before throwing it out. How's that?"

Wanting to be helpful, Allie agreed, but vowed to err on the side of caution. If she had the least feeling that any single piece of paper might be of value, she would make sure not to discard it. This time she would *think* before she acted.

Brianna showed her a large storage room off the office. Between overfull cardboard boxes and old metal filing cabinets, there was barely room to move. Layers of dust covered every horizontal surface, and the room smelled musty.

"See what I mean? This place hasn't had a cleaning in years." Brianna opened the top drawer of a filing cabinet. "Some of these records go back to Cord's grandfather's time. At the very least, they ought to be placed in permanent storage somewhere, not kept here in the office."

Allie eyed the chaotic files. "Perhaps if I sort them into three piles—those I believe should be kept, rec-

ords I am not sure should be saved, and whatever I
believe might be discarded without creating harm.''

''That would be perfect. I really appreciate your
help.''

Brianna found her a clean cardboard box that had
once held her computer, and Allie carried it into the
storeroom. No question, this was going to be an all-
day project.

CORD RETURNED from moving cattle to a dark, eerily
quiet house. The stove was cold. The coffeepot
looked as though it hadn't been refilled since morning.

He knew Brianna had an appointment with the accountant in Austin and was planning to do some shopping. But Allie ought to be here.

Dread twisted his gut. She'd left without saying
goodbye. Maybe she'd gotten a lift from Brianna to
the Austin airport. By now she was probably winging
her way back to Munir.

Not that he blamed her. He'd been giving her a
damn hard time. Resuming her life as a princess must
have seemed like a better choice than hanging around
with him.

He walked through the kitchen and dining room,
into the great room with its Western motif oak furniture, leather couches and original oil paintings of
rodeo riders and cattle roundups on the wall. Pictures
and furnishings his mother had selected.

She'd left him, too.

His chest tightened. He'd known all along that Allie would leave. No reason why it should bother him now.

Determined to ignore the ache of loss, he was about to return to the kitchen to fix himself a sandwich when he noticed a sliver of light coming from the office.

"Brianna? Are you here?" he called.

When there was no response, he followed the light to its source, which wasn't the office but the adjacent storage room, its door standing wide-open, the contents looking as though they'd been ransacked.

"What the hell!" he muttered. He'd have to call the sheriff to report the vandalism. There wasn't a damn thing of any value in there, so robbery couldn't be—

He halted abruptly at the doorway. Allie sat cross-legged on the floor, surrounded by piles of papers, an old photo album open in her lap. His relief at seeing her was tempered by a troubling suspicion that Mischief had struck again.

"What in heaven's name are you up to?"

She started, then look up at him with eyes filled with tears. She smiled weakly. "I did not hear you come home."

He hunkered down beside her. "What's wrong?"

"N-nothing. It's just all so wonderful."

Confusion tightened his forehead. "Beyond the total mess you've made, what's so wonderful?"

She made a vague gesture that encompassed the entire room. "Here is the history of the Flying Ace— of all of Texas. Those people who fought the Indians and helped make Texas an independent country. The women who baked bread and bore their children here. How much it cost to buy a cow and how much it could be sold for. There is more than a hundred years of history here.''

He'd never actually gone through all the records his father had kept. Certainly hadn't troubled himself with what had gone on a hundred years ago. Allie was acting like she'd entered a holy place or a museum.

She caressed the photo album in her lap. "And this is your history. You were a beautiful baby, Cord Brannigan.''

"Oh, shoot, my baby pictures!" Somewhere in there he knew she'd find one of those bare bottom shots he'd just as soon forget.

"Your mother must have loved you very much to have saved so many memories of you.''

"Right. That's why she took off when I was twelve, because she loved me so much.''

"You must not doubt her love.'' She flipped back through the pages to the beginning of the album. "See? Here she is holding you. Look at her eyes and tell me what you see.''

He didn't want to look. "Nothing. Nothing at all.''

"There are others.''

She turned page after page, revealing memories from the past. His first birthday, his mother laughing as he stuffed a piece of chocolate cake into his mouth. His mother holding him on a merry-go-round at the fair when he'd been about two. His first day of school, holding his mother's hand. Report cards tucked between the pages. Him in his Little League uniform.

There were snapshots of the three of them, too. His mother and father with Cord in the middle, everybody smiling at the camera.

The memories were like a summer heat wave, pressing him down, making it difficult to draw a breath, and he looked away.

Allie caressed his cheek, her hand cool. "Tell me about your mother."

"What's to tell?"

"Whatever is your best memory."

He didn't want to think about any of that, yet the image that popped into his mind was so vivid he couldn't ignore it. He swallowed hard before he could form the words.

"For a while there was an old table set up on the patio. It was made out of one-by-six planks. Over the years it had warped, probably from being left out in the rain. I don't know what it was supposed to be used for—maybe a serving table for barbecues—but one summer my mother and I used it for a Ping-Pong table."

In spite of himself, he smiled at the memory. "That fool ball would land in one of the cracks and bounce off in some screwy direction. We never knew which way it was going to fly. Mom got the giggles so bad I almost wet my pants."

"And you have other happy memories?" Allie asked softly.

This time the memory came more quickly and with

less pain. "Yeah. We used to go on picnics at the creek in the south forty. One time we went and didn't know Dad had moved the bulls to that pasture. Ol' Bart's granddad put down his head and charged us. Mom scooped me up and ran for the pickup. Never knew she could make tracks so fast."

Shoving his fingers through his hair, Cord savored the memory for a moment. "She stuffed me in the cab, then turned on that ol' bull and went screaming after him. Scared him nearly to death. He never bothered us again."

"You see, it is as I have said." Allie took his hand, brushing a kiss on his knuckles. "Your mother loved you very much."

"Then why did she leave?"

"What passes between a husband and wife, no one can know. But I am sure she did what she thought was best for you."

It hadn't felt like it at the time. It still didn't, which didn't say much about Cord's ability to put the past behind him. But he had to give Allie credit for trying to make him feel better about his mother leaving him.

Standing, he pulled Allie to her feet with him. "Now, you want to tell me what the heck is going on here?"

"Your sister asked me to help her sort through all these old records and discard—"

"You're throwing away all this stuff?" In the mountains of papers she'd piled on the floor, he knew damn well there were important records. It would be just like Mischief to throw away something crucial like the original brand registration for the ranch or his birth certificate.

"No, not at all. Only this one small stack of old catalogs seems of no value."

"How would you know what's valuable in this mess?"

She did her haughty head toss, her dark hair flying behind her shoulder, and narrowed her eyes. "We have a very fine ancient history museum in Munir filled with antiquities, and I have worked many long hours with the curator. It is tedious work, but very rewarding. And this—" she made a dramatic sweep with her hand "—is history. The records need to be cataloged and properly stored, not in simple cardboard boxes. University researchers in American history will need access to these records. They are invaluable in the study of ordinary people and how they lived their lives. Entire books can be written based on this material. To discard any of it would be criminal. I think you should hire your own curator. It will take years to sift through the wealth of information."

Cord laughed. He hadn't seen her worked up over anything as much as she was about a ton of musty old papers.

"You are one amazing woman, Mischief." And then he did the most natural thing in the world.

He bent his head and kissed her.

He'd meant the kiss to be brief, but the contact jolted him. Lifting his head, he saw the same startled reaction in Allie's dark eyes, the same yearning need that had been swirling in his midsection since she'd arrived at the Flying Ace. A need that kept building like a tornado rolling across the hill country, devouring everything in its path.

When he lowered his head again it wasn't a slow and lazy kiss, but one that demanded she respond with the same enthusiasm she'd expressed for dried-up bits of paper. His mouth was hot and hungry, possessing hers. He plunged his tongue inside. Her taste was full of sweet sex appeal, her scent promising sultry tropical secrets. She permeated his senses.

She made a sound of wonder, wrapping her arms around his neck, giving back as good as she got. Her body moved to match itself to his, her breasts flattening against his chest, her pelvis rocking against the hard ridge of his arousal. He cupped her bottom, lifting her off her feet, and she wrapped her legs around his waist.

What had started as a kiss turned into a need for something far more elemental. More essential. And Cord had this crazy notion of taking her right here in the storage room on a pile of musty old papers. Except he didn't want to stop kissing her. Not even for as long as it would take to strip her of every stitch of clothing she had on.

He felt himself trembling. His knees threatened to buckle, and it wasn't because she was too heavy. In fact, she was as light as a feather. A weight he could carry forever.

Right into his bedroom.

Turning, he started to do just that, but then heard Brianna's voice calling from the front of the house.

"Anybody home?"

He groaned and so did Allie.

She buried her head against his chest as he lowered her to her feet. She rocked slightly. He braced her while trying to catch his own breath. What he didn't need was for Brianna to catch them like this.

"I'll be right there," he called to Brianna.

Drawing another shuddering breath, Allie stepped away from him. Her eyes were as dark as a moonless sky, her cheeks flushed, her delicate lips swollen.

"I was afraid you would never kiss me again," she whispered.

He arched a brow in surprise. "I think you can count on it happening again, Mischief. Unless you have some serious objection."

Wordlessly, she shook her head.

Cord figured it would be a good thirty minutes before he could face his sister without the telltale evidence of what he'd been up to apparent to even a mildly observant person.

Brianna was a lot more perceptive than that.

Chapter Nine

Still a little weak in the knees, Allie stepped away from Cord as Brianna walked into the office, a stack of mail in her hand. Her gaze darted from Allie to her brother and then to the piles of papers heaped up in the storage room.

"Hi! Uh, how'd the sorting project go?"

"Fine." Allie's face felt as though it were on fire. For that matter, her whole body did. She was confident Cord had been ready to do far more than kiss her had Brianna not returned, and she rued the interruption.

Acting casual, Cord sauntered over to his desk and picked up a letter opener, drumming it on his palm. "She wants to turn the storage room into a museum."

Brianna's eyes widened. "A museum? I was planning to burn most of that old stuff."

"No, no, you must not do that. There is a journal of a woman who came here by covered wagon. She fought the Indians. Two of her children died of diphtheria. It would be a tragedy to lose that part of history, however sad it might be."

Shaking her head, Brianna said, "In that case, we're going to have to build another room onto the house. I just ordered three more filing cabinets to be delivered. I got a really good price."

"We'll deal with it somehow," Cord said, not making eye contact with either his sister or Allie.

Brianna continued to study the two of them suspiciously. "I got a call early this morning from the attorney in New Hampshire. My aunt's probate is all sewed up and the escrow papers on her house are ready to be signed. I made flight reservations for tomorrow."

"That soon, huh?" Cord commented.

"Aunt Elaine died more than a year ago. It seems like the paperwork has taken forever, and I'm anxious to get it over with. Get that part of my life behind me."

"I can understand that." He stuffed his hands in his pockets. "Well, I haven't had anything to eat since morning. I'm going to see what's in the refrigerator."

Brianna nailed Allie with a questioning look. "You haven't fixed dinner?"

"It must have slipped my mind."

No way was Allie going to confess what had distracted her from her domestic chores, beyond her excavation of the storage room's contents. Cord's sister was welcome to speculate, but Allie didn't intend to provide any details.

And she felt only a little guilty that Brianna would be gone from the house for a few days. Cord's promise of yet another kiss would be much better enjoyed if they were on their own—without a chaperon.

And it had been a promise, she was sure. A titillating pledge that had made her heart take flight on the wings of excitement. Even now she could barely stop herself from running after Cord, claiming the kiss this very moment and demanding he keep on kissing her until she had her fill. Which would take a very long while. Possibly years.

DURING THE PAST YEAR, Cord had gotten used to having Brianna around the house. She was pleasant, unobtrusive company. A good conversationalist who knew when to be silent, too.

He never thought he'd be quite so happy to have her leave for a few days.

He waved goodbye as she drove away from the house, then turned to Allie. She looked terrific this morning, with her gleaming hair held back by a silver headband that caught the sun like a crown. Her cheeks captured the soft rose of sunrise; her dark eyes glistened with a hint of excitement and anticipation. A princess in jeans.

"Guess I'd better check with the hands, see that everything is under control." For Cord, work had to come before pleasure, but this morning work wouldn't take long.

"I was thinking I might start cataloging some of your historical records. Is there a Texas museum?"

"Sure. A bunch of them. But don't get too involved this morning."

"No?" Amusement arched her brows. "There is something else you need of me today?"

Oh, yeah, and he needed it badly. He gauged the possibility of showing her what he had in mind before checking with Pablo and his ranch hands, but the hum of an approaching vehicle distracted him. A dusty SUV came into view. The driver honked and waved, then drove on toward the barn and corrals.

Cord grimaced as his plans for the morning blew up in the cloud of dust that trailed the SUV.

"That is a friend of yours?" Allie asked.

"Hannah Clark Coleman, Alex's wife and the local veterinarian. She took over her father's practice a year or so ago. If she's here, chances are Pablo called her because we've got a sick animal."

"Oh, dear."

Yeah. Oh, dear, was right. "I've gotta go check it out. It won't take long."

With a wry smile, she slipped her arm through his. "In my country we have an ancient and very wise saying." She rattled off a string of words in her own language that he had no hope of understanding.

"What's that mean?"

"Timing is everything. I will come with you to see that the sick animal is well cared for."

She gave a lighthearted, feminine laugh that had him gritting his teeth and wishing he owned a pair of jeans a couple of sizes larger.

IN THE STABLE, the woman carrying a black bag had honey-blond hair a shade or two darker than

Brianna's. She questioned the ranch hand in a way that indicated she knew exactly what she was doing.

What surprised Allie were the twin babies the veterinarian carried in a double sling across her chest.

Gracious, but the Coleman family produced a good many sets of twins. In Allie's country they were rare; here the Colemans multiplied like jackrabbits.

"What happened?" Cord asked of Ty, who was talking to the veterinarian.

"I had Sweet Sue out checking fences near Highway 73 yesterday. She picked up a nail, probably from the construction crew that was working nearby." Ty lifted his hat and scratched at his head, his forehead furrowed with worry. "I pulled it out soon as I felt her go lame. But she still wasn't right this morning. Pablo said I should call Hannah."

Cord nodded his approval.

"Just as well you did," Hannah said. "From the way she's favoring her right foreleg, keeping her weight on her hind legs, I'd say the front one's abscessing. But I need to take a closer look."

Allie stepped forward. "Would it help if I held the babies for you?"

The veterinarian smiled in relief. "You're Leila, aren't you?"

Allie felt a guilty blush stain her cheeks.

"Oh, don't worry that folks have been talking about you. The Desert Rose is like a *very* small town. I just heard that you were helping Cord and his sister while Maria was away."

"Yes, that is true," Allie muttered, hating that her lies had spread so far.

"Usually I don't bring the boys along on house calls, but Alex—my husband—was off somewhere and no one seemed available to baby-sit." She lifted one of the babies from the sling. "This one's Ryan. Can you manage two at once?"

"I think so." Her tension easing, Allie looked around for somewhere to sit, and spotted an old leather chair with the stuffing sticking out. She carried Ryan to the chair, sat down, and Hannah handed her the other twin, Justin. Mittens came bounding out from behind a bale of hay to investigate what was happening.

"How old are the babies?" Allie asked.

"Five months, but like most twins they're a little small for their age."

"They are beautiful, both of them." They were identical with caps of mocha-brown hair and mouths so tiny they naturally formed an *O*.

"If they start rooting around looking for a snack," Hannah said, "tell them to wait. This might take awhile. I may have to lance the abscess." With a smile, she gave Allie two pacifiers. "This will help."

It took a moment to get comfortable with a baby in each arm, but Allie found *two* precious bundles were even more delightful than one. Mittens hopped up onto the back of the chair, batting at Allie's headband, and she shooed her away. The kitten scurried after a real or imagined bug, sending dust motes into the air.

In Allie's arms, Justin stirred in his sleep. She rocked back and forth, humming a traditional Munir lullaby her own mother had sung to her. Allie hadn't thought of that in years, hadn't known she could recall it, and she smiled at the distant memory.

Another memory surfaced, too—a dream she'd once had of bearing her own babies and holding them in her arms. But when she'd been betrothed to Sardar that dream had seemed like a nightmare. His were not the children she wanted to hold and cuddle.

Instead she wanted to bear the children of a man she loved.

Hannah was working in the stall with the mare, Ty had gone off to check on something, and when Allie glanced up from the babies, only Cord was there.

Her breath caught at the look in his eyes. Heated, to be sure. Sensual. But more than that. A feeling swept through her that could only be described as the way the leaders of a camel caravan must have felt in ancient times when they finally had their destination in sight.

She had at last come home.

Tears pricked at the back of her eyes. "Would you like to hold one of the babies?" *Would you let me have your babies, dozens of them?*

He shook his head. "You're doing fine. Let's not rock the boat."

Pain pierced her heart. Had he heard her question, which she thought surely she had said aloud? Was he saying that he did not want her to mother his children? Or simply that he did not want to hold a twin?

Perhaps, as a man, he could not hear her dreams as clearly she wished him to.

Hannah came back out of the stall, wiping her hands on a clean towel. ''You'll have to be sure that abscess keeps draining. I'll come back day after tomorrow to see how it's going.''

Cord turned his attention to the veterinarian. ''Thanks, Hannah. Maybe we ought to put up some signs along the fence line that say don't toss nails into the pasture.''

''It's even worse in town. Can't tell you the things that get stuck in horses' hooves if they're ridden in the streets. It's enough to keep me employed for years.'' She smiled down at her babies, sleeping peacefully in Allie's arms. ''Let me get washed up and I'll take the twins off your hands.''

''Do not hurry,'' Allie urged, knowing she'd miss the sweet warmth of the infants when they were gone.

Cord helped Hannah pack up her doctor's case. Something had passed between him and Allie when she'd been holding the babies. Something that took him beyond his nearly continual state of lust when he was around her.

Something about motherhood that was more enduring than a roll in the hay.

The thought that when she returned to Munir she'd mother another man's babies gave him a sharp stab of regret, more irritating than it should have been.

He shoved the thought aside and forcefully unclenched his teeth. He needed to keep his emotions out of the mix when it came to Allie. She'd never intended to stay long in Texas. That much was obvious from the temporary "loan" of a servant her brother had arranged. No doubt she was here on a lark, slumming with the commoners.

Which didn't stop Cord from wanting her, not for a minute. But it did mean he had to keep his head on straight. No commitments. No investment in the outcome except for two adults enjoying the pleasure of each other's bodies.

Given his experience with women, he knew the price he'd pay if he didn't stick with the rules of survival he'd learned the hard way.

Hannah loaded up her twins in the dual carrier, and Cord carried her medical case out to her SUV. Allie came along, still cooing over the babies.

"Thanks for coming by," he said to Hannah.

"No problem. The way things are going, I figure in another year or two, I'll have the boys trained as veterinarian assistants, they will have gone out on so many calls with me."

Cord laughed, then stepped back from the truck as she drove away.

Releasing a long sigh, Allie asked, "Do you have any twins in your family?"

"Not that I know about."

"What a shame."

Cord did a double take, but he wasn't interested in discussing babies or his family history. He intended to return to plan A, now that Brianna had left for New Hampshire and Hannah was all through doctoring the horse.

He'd have Allie—on his own terms, without getting his heart involved.

Taking her hand, he laced his fingers through hers and tugged her closer. "It seems to me we began something last night that we didn't have a chance to finish."

Her dark eyes studied him a moment before understanding appeared, then they began to sparkle. "Naturally, you are referring to sorting all the valuable documents I discovered?"

"Not exactly." From the corner of his eye, he spotted Joe sauntering in his direction. With a discreet wave, he tried to warn his hired hand away.

Joe didn't get the message. "Hey, boss, you want I should take care of that there rooster now?"

Cord stifled a groan. "Sure. Now would be fine."

"I'll jest go get the ax then."

Allie's tender expression vanished in a heartbeat, and she pulled back from Cord. "What rooster is Joe talking about?"

"You know, the rooster in the chicken coop. That's where most roosters live. He's getting pretty old and it's time to—"

"Joe is not going to lay a hand on him, not while there is still breath in my body." Pulling her hand free, she went running toward the coop.

Dumbstruck, Cord tried to make sense of what had gone wrong with plan A—again!

"Wait!" He raced after her. "Mischief, what the hell are you up to now?"

She reached the chicken coop a few steps before

him, turned and blocked the doorway. "The rooster is a brave and courageous animal who protects his women. I will not let you kill him."

"He's a damn rooster who's getting cranky in his old age. He belongs in a pot before he gets too tough—"

"No!" she cried. "He is bossy and arrogant, but so are you. How would you like it if some giant came along and decided to put *you* in a pot?"

"I'm not bossy," he protested. Allie was the darndest woman he'd ever met, getting emotionally attached to a damn chicken. Despite her high-and-mighty upbringing, she was standing there in all of her feminine glory defending one of the dumbest creatures on God's green earth. A man had to respect that kind of passion.

And want some of that passion to be directed toward him.

Joe showed up carrying the ax over his shoulder and looking about as confused as Cord felt. "You want I should do it, boss, or not?"

Inside the chicken coop, the rooster crowed and the hens took up his complaint.

Allie launched herself at Cord, pounding her small fists on his chest. "Don't do it! Please don't let him—"

"Hush, Mischief." The only way he could stop her from hurting herself was to wrap his arms around her, hold her tight. "The bird gets executive clemency, okay?" With a flick of his head, he gestured for Joe to forget the rooster. "He'll keep on crowing for as long as you want."

Sobbing, Allie mashed her face against his shoulder. "Thank you," she whispered, her words muffled, her delicate body shaking.

Determined not to lose sight of plan A again, Cord lifted her in his arms and carried her back toward the house. Joe gave him an odd look, which he ignored. If he had his way, a tornado wasn't going to stop him this time. The only thing that would slow him down would be for Allie to say no.

He couldn't bear the thought of that. The fly on his jeans wouldn't be able to handle the stress, either.

Slowly, Allie became aware of Cord carrying her. The masculine scent of him mixing with the perfume of detergent on his shirt where she pressed her face drew a feminine response from her. The muscular strength of his arms as he carried her easily made her want to surrender to his every command. As he walked purposefully toward the house, the sun beat down on them, but the greater heat she felt came from inside.

He was going to kiss her again. And perhaps more.

She gave a fleeting thought to the custom of arriving at her marriage bed still a virgin, and immediately discarded the notion. She would go there with carnal knowledge of Cord, grateful to have that memory to last her a lifetime.

Cooler air washed over her as he entered the back door to the kitchen, and in the silent room she could hear them both breathing hard. He lowered her feet to the floor, but her arms remained wrapped around his neck. His eyes were the deepest green she'd ever seen them. Almost black. The look they held was meant only for her.

Slowly, he removed the silver band from her hair and set it on the kitchen table. Her hair fell loose past her shoulders.

She shivered in anticipation.

"Baby, if the phone rings, ignore it. Ignore everything but this." He lowered his head to kiss her.

Masterfully, he claimed her mouth, and time stood still, spinning out on threads of golden pleasure. Melting her bones until her strength vanished. Only sensation remained. The coffee-flavored taste of him. His callused palm skimming her cheek, his fingers tangling in her hair. The hard ridge at the front of his jeans pressing against her belly.

Kissing was a wonderful adventure, but she wanted more.

"Cord? Can we—"

"I'm counting on it."

She nodded, her heart pounding in her ears so loudly she thought surely he could hear the pulsing beat. Cord's kisses created a maelstrom of need she'd never realized could be so compelling.

He lifted her, aligning their bodies so his arousal was right where she wanted to feel it. Instinctively, she wrapped her legs around his waist. Shifting her position, she felt desire lance through her, and she cried out at the pleasurable sensation.

"Easy, Mischief. I'd like us to get as far as the bedroom."

They journeyed through the house, kiss by kiss, Cord nibbling on her lips, she nipping at his corded throat while he watched where they were going.

In his bedroom, a ceiling fan lazily circulated the air above the king-size bed she had previously admired. The patterned spread looked inviting, but he tossed the covers aside in favor of smooth percale sheets.

"Let me look at you," he pleaded. His fingers trembled at her midriff as he pulled her T-shirt off over her head, and he drew an audible breath. "You are so beautiful."

She'd had no idea how a man's rough-textured hands would feel on her breasts as he learned their size and shape. At first she wished her breasts were larger, more appealing. But when Cord smiled, she knew he was pleased with all she had to offer.

Closing her eyes, she gave herself over to the delight of his thumbs scraping over her nipples, puckering them to hard nubs.

"That's very nice," she whispered.

"It's going to get nicer, Mischief. I promise."

She could barely imagine how that would be true until she toed off her boots, allowing him to lower her jeans, tugging them off. He urged her down onto the bed, the sheets cold beneath her back, the fan chilling the sheen of perspiration that coated her skin. When he caressed the flimsy fabric of her panties, she bucked beneath his hand.

"Oh, my…" she gasped.

"Perfect."

For a big man, he was gentle, caressing her totally without haste. He nuzzled her breasts. Laved the nipples. Drew them into his mouth. Her body arched uncontrollably against his hand when he probed with his fingers at that secret spot that ached for his touch.

No man could have treated her with more care. Handling her as though she were the most priceless object in the universe. Worshipping her in ways she had only vaguely been aware were possible.

She had no idea when he removed her panties—or his own clothes. She only knew seeing him naked and fully aroused thrilled her beyond measure, and at the same time frightened her.

He kissed her lips, her face, the juncture of her thighs.

"Don't be afraid," he murmured as the shock of it rippled through her body.

"I'm not," she lied. Or perhaps it wasn't a lie at all. With Cord, she would have no fear. He would not hurt her however vulnerable she might be.

He fumbled with something from the bed table drawer, then knelt above her, nudging her legs apart.

"I think I've wanted to do this since the first day you arrived at the Flying Ace."

She closed her eyes, waiting. Trembling.

"Look at me, Princess. I want to see your eyes when I'm inside you."

She watched as he probed gently, moving in and out only centimeters at a time until she craved more of him. Was willing to risk everything to feel his length deep within her. Frantic, she arched up to him in welcome.

He held her off, pausing before entering her with care. Even so, the pain came sharply as he finally accepted her invitation, but it faded with equal speed. He held her tightly, waiting before he stretched and filled her more fully. And at last, she was one with Cord. Slowly they began to move together.

It was like a journey to some desert mountaintop, searching for the peak that was hidden in mystery and shrouded by tales told in whispers within the women's quarters. She let Cord guide her, followed his rhythm, clung to him as he took her perilously close to an edge she couldn't see.

With a gasp, she reached the pinnacle. Sunshine burst through her, and she cried out in celebration. An instant later, when his shudder of pleasure joined hers, she seemed to fly past that highest peak into a world where she was weightless, floating back to the lush valley below, held firmly in Cord's embrace.

Time drifted in that dreamless way until she turned onto her side, cuddling against his length. As he dozed on his back, one arm still wrapped around her shoulders, she gave free rein to her urge to examine the man who had so tenderly taken her virginity.

The sun had left a tan line where he wore his hat low on his forehead. His eyelashes swept in half circles against his cheek, lashes unfairly long for such a ruggedly handsome man. His hair curled slightly at his nape; his perfectly formed ear fit close to his head.

After holding Hannah's twins today, Allie could easily imagine cuddling two little boys with Cord's saddle-brown hair, and his intriguing eyes filled with greens and golds, surrounded by equally long lashes.

But that was not to be, she reminded herself. Her life and the man she was pledged to marry were in Munir.

Opening his eyes a slit, Cord asked, "You planning to look at me all day?"

"Quite possibly." She smiled. It might be years and years before she got her fill of him, although she did not have that choice to make.

He grunted an unintelligible sound.

"How did you break your nose?"

His forehead creased and his eyes opened more widely. "When I was about fifteen, I took a header off a bronc and landed face first in the dirt."

"Oh, dear..." With her fingertip she traced the tiny scar beneath his right eye. "And this? Also from the bronc?"

"Nope. That was Cade Coleman's doing."

"He hit you? I thought you were friends."

"We were. He got a rocket-launched airplane for Christmas one year. I had the poor timing to step in front of it when he lit it off."

"You could have been blinded," she said with some alarm.

"Fortunately, my head did his plane more damage than the other way around." Raising up on one arm, Cord smoothed her tangled hair back from her face, studying her with a serious air. "I thought this would probably be your first time. Are you okay with what just happened?''

"More than okay." She blinked in surprise. "You knew I had never... Did I do something wrong?"

He chuckled, a low rumble in his chest. "You were perfect. No man could ask for a more responsive woman than you were. Absolutely perfect."

Caressing his face, filled with delight at his words of praise, she let her fingers slide into the thickness of his hair. "I am glad you were my first."

He closed his eyes and exhaled slowly. "Let's see, I guess we could get up and do our chores, like this was just another day on the ranch. Or..."

"Or stay right here in bed all day?"

He laughed. "Mischief, I have the feeling you could wear out a man without even half trying."

"Not such a strong, powerful man as you, I am sure," she teased.

"If that's the case, I've got an idea. Seems to me when you first got here I promised you a ride on one of my cutting horses. You still game for it?"

Though surprised by his suggestion, she had no desire to reject a chance to see the rest of the ranch. "Oh, yes. I would like that very much."

"Good. Then let's fix us a picnic. I'll take you out to the creek and we'll go skinny-dipping in the ol' swimming hole."

Her eyes widened. "Skinny-dipping?"

"You'll love it." He nuzzled her neck right beneath her ear, a particularly sensitive spot he'd discovered earlier. "An unforgettable experience. I promise."

IN MUNIR, Sheikh Ashraf Bahram dismissed his advisors and excused his personal secretary for the evening.

His schedule since his return from America had been hectic. Although Munir was a small oil producer compared to many of their neighboring countries, Rafe still needed to attend meetings and keep in almost daily contact with their leaders.

To add to his usual workload, in the past week an oil tanker sailing under Munir's colors had run aground in the Gulf of Oman. There had been fear of a leak, an ecological disaster. Negotiations with the Oman authorities had been heated and not entirely cordial.

Fortunately, a crisis had been averted and the situation returned to normal with no serious damage done to the Gulf of Oman's shoreline.

Finding himself with a few free minutes, Rafe thought he would visit his sister to see how she and her plans for her wedding were faring. Though it was past suppertime, he was confident Aliah and her ladies-in-waiting would not yet have retired for the night.

At the end of a long, tiled hallway with alabaster walls, he rapped his knuckles on the heavy wooden door to the women's quarters. A moment later, a young girl whose name he didn't recall opened the door for him.

"Your highness?"

"I would like to have words with my sister."

The girl lowered her gaze to the floor. "Princess Aliah is not here, my lord."

"She is out somewhere?" It seemed an odd time for her to be away, but Aliah had never been predictable. And she did have friends all around the city.

"Do you know when she will return?"

Without looking at him, the girl vigorously shook her head. "I am sorry, my lord."

A troubling feeling crept down his spine. "Perhaps one of the older women would have the information I seek."

The girl took his words as a cue to flee back into the women's quarters.

With increasing impatience, Rafe waited until Leila appeared at the door, looking pale and troubled.

"Leila, what is going on? I was looking for—" A bolt of awareness shot through him. "You did not remain in Texas?"

She hung her head. "No, my lord."

He clenched his teeth to halt a string of epithets that threatened to erupt. "Aliah took your place." It wasn't a question. What Aliah had done was suddenly obvious. And unforgivable. At the time, he'd sensed his sister had been up to something when she'd asked that her closest lady-in-waiting remain for a time with Cord Brannigan. Rafe should have relied on his instincts.

Struck dumb by the truth he had discovered, he only stared as Leila nodded.

Whirling, Rafe marched back down the long corridor to his own quarters, where he roused his private secretary, who was preparing for bed.

"Raul, order my plane to be ready at first light."

"Sir?" Caught off guard, he tugged his nightshirt down over his shoulders. "Where will you be going?"

"America." He spat out the word. "To Texas to bring back my wayward sister."

Chapter Ten

Stunted oak trees and junipers punctuated the rolling hills southwest of the ranch house, and the grass grew lush in the low-lying gullies. At midday, the hot sun wilted what few wildflowers remained this late in the season. The air, heavy with humidity, tried to do the same to Allie's spirits, but failed.

Riding comfortably astride a buckskin quarter horse with a white blaze on its face, Allie felt buoyed by the intimacies she had shared with the man who rode beside her. Her blood warmed, humming through her veins with the new knowledge she had gained. Nothing she had heard in the women's quarters compared to the reality of loving a man.

Loving Cord.

He sat his mount well, his back straight, his hands easy on the reins, his hat tilted low enough to keep the sun from his face. Yet she sensed an alertness about him. A passion for his land, perhaps. An awareness that he was as much a part of the land as the trees and grass that grew here. Each leaf, each blade of grass was his.

The sigh that came unexpectedly was filled with regret that she could not claim that same sense of belonging.

"Bored?" he asked.

"No, not at all. The countryside is beautiful."

"Different than Munir, I suppose."

"Much. We have only a few oases that would compare to this, and they are small."

"Not to mention they've got palm trees, not oaks."

"True." She laughed. She wished she could tell him more about her life in Munir, that she was a princess whose days were often restricted within the palace walls. Tell him that she cherished the freedom of these wide-open spaces, of vistas that went on to the horizon, more than most women would. Let him know she would soon have to return to that constricted life and would miss him terribly.

She wished she could be honest with Cord. But however kind and gentle he had been with her, she still feared he would send back to Munir as quickly as a jackrabbit darted from one hiding place to another if he knew the truth.

She swallowed the despair that rose in her throat and the guilt for her deceit. For now she would concentrate on the picnic they would share.

They had filled his saddlebags with hard-boiled eggs, roast beef sandwiches, potato chips, bite-size pieces of cheese, grapes, oranges and a bottle of red wine. In her view, a royal banquet fit for a sheikh.

Or for lovers.

She grinned at the thought. Never in all her twenty-two years had she imagined she would have a lover. Until now.

"You want to let me in on the joke?" he asked.

She tossed her head with mock disdain. "Perhaps when we reach our destination, I will show you exactly what I was thinking about."

He eyed her from beneath the brim of his hat. "I like the sound of that. The ol' swimming hole is over the next hill." He shot her a challenging look. "How 'bout I race you there? Unless you're afraid you won't be able to stay on your horse."

Accepting his dare, she spurred her mare into a gallop. Her quick action caught him off guard, gaining her horse a few strides before Cord reacted. But his gelding was bigger and stronger, with longer legs than her mare, and he caught up quickly. They sped up the gently rolling hillside, her horse struggling courageously to stay in the lead.

As they crested the ridge, she laughed aloud in unadulterated joy. Never had she felt more alive. More free. Deep in her heart, she prayed that the day her brother discovered her absence would never come—a futile hope, she knew, but one she harbored with all the intensity she could muster.

Cord touched his heels to his mount one more time. Grinning, he raced past Allie and her mare. Her laughter rippled through the air like water tumbling and bouncing along a creek bed, cascading with happy abandon toward the lake. No inhibitions or royal obligations constrained her enjoyment of the moment.

She'd been like that as they made love, too. No holding back. Giving her all. A woman like that was a treasure worth more than a palace filled with gold and diamonds.

If a man could keep her as his own.

The creek that ran through the Flying Ace meandered where the hills dipped together, a winding path between boulders and sandy, rock-strewn banks that were overrun during heavy rains. Cottonwood trees sank their roots into the moist soil near the water, their dusty leaves casting shadows that rippled across the slow-moving current. The air had always been cooler here, fresher than at the ranch house.

Cord dismounted, grabbing Allie's reins as she raced up beside him and tugged her horse to a stop. God, she was beautiful when riding at full gallop, her white Stetson flying behind her head, her strong legs pumping in the stirrups. A woman as hard to corral as a wild mustang, and all the more valuable because of her spirit.

"You're a pretty good rider for someone who lost control of her mount and needed to be rescued only ten days ago."

"This animal is much better trained than that horse was."

He placed his hands on her midriff, and she slid from the saddle in a graceful movement, her arms curling around his neck. Her lithe body curved against his as he lowered her to her feet.

"Don't let Mac Coleman hear you malign his livestock. He prides himself on having the best-trained horses in Texas.''

"Perhaps his pride is undeserved.''

Unable to resist, Cord brushed a kiss to her lips. He might have lingered longer but her horse, excited from the race, tried to dance away from him.

"Easy, girl.'' The mare tossed her head when Cord didn't release his grip on the bridle. "I'll take the horses downstream for a drink. You find us a nice spot to stretch out for lunch.'' *And anything else we might think of doing,* he mentally added.

He led the horses to water, then tethered them well away from the creek and came back to Allie, carrying the saddlebags and a blanket, which he spread beneath a cottonwood.

She'd already pulled off her boots to dangle her toes in the stream, where nature had strewn boulders to create a low dam that backed up the creek into a pool. With her hat tossed carelessly aside, her long hair glistened in the sunlight as though brushed with diamond dust.

"You ready for a swim? Or do you want to eat first?'' he asked.

A teasing smile curled her lips. "I did not bring a swimsuit.''

"That's the whole idea of skinny-dipping.'' Unbuttoning his shirt, he tugged it from his jeans and tossed it on the blanket. "We don't need suits.''

"No one will see us?''

He undid his silver belt buckle. "Nope. This is the Flying Ace's own private pool, and my ranch hands are all busy somewhere else.'' Something he'd made sure of before they'd left the main ranch.

"And it is safe to swim here?"

"Been doing it since I was a kid.'' He and the Coleman boys had learned to swim here, had had their first taste of beer—and their first hangovers—here.

Her gaze focused on him with avid interest as he unsnapped his jeans. "To do such a thing makes me feel very wicked."

"Guess I could go in alone if you're chicken.''

"Being chicken is not good, is it?"

"Definitely not.'' He sat down long enough to pull off his boots and ease out of his jeans. He was already aroused and wasn't sure the cold water would change that much. "You coming?"

"I have heard it said that it is not wise to swim alone.'' She shed her blouse, stood up and wiggled out of her designer jeans. "I would not want to put you in danger by allowing you to swim by yourself."

Cord knew he was in a greater danger than drowning in the ol' swimming hole. The sight of Allie standing in the sunlight stark naked was like seeing a magnificent porcelain statue created by the finest artist in the world. Her breasts peaked, high and proud. Her waist narrowed above the swell of her hips. Between her legs, a patch of pecan-brown curls veiled the womanly secrets he wanted to explore again.

"On second thought, maybe we could come up with another choice besides swimming or eating,'' he said.

She laughed in delight, lifted her arms above her head, arched her body and dived into the pool, barely raising a splash as she entered the water.

"Damn," he muttered, and grinning, went in after her.

Allie folded her legs to slow her descent, twisted and stroked for the opposite side of the pool. The icy cold water chilled her flesh, but not the heat of desire. She didn't want to rush their lovemaking. Nor did she want to make life too easy for Cord. He'd have his way with her soon enough—and she with him.

For now, she wanted to stretch out the moments they shared together, suspend time, if she could. Ignore the mental image of a clock ticking much too fast with the final minutes and seconds catching up with them.

Popping up, she drew in a quick breath of air, tossing her wet hair away from her face.

Cord was nowhere in sight.

She spun around, treading water as she searched beneath the surface for him. The way the light glistened, dancing across the pool, it was difficult to see anything beneath her. He could be—

Something grabbed her ankle. She gasped as he pulled her under, submerging her.

His laughing face was in front of hers, his hands now on her rib cage, his thumbs flicking across her taut nipples. She struggled, trying to pull away. Trying not to laugh. He kissed her, their breaths mingling, bubbles floating up beside them. She plunged her fingers through his hair, thick strands capturing her, just as he had snared her.

Her lungs began to burn as he kicked his feet, sending them upward, their legs entangled, and they burst above the surface, both gasping for air.

"No fair!" she cried, drawing in precious oxygen, yet unable to stifle her laughter. Or her exhilaration at the teasing fun of being with the man she loved.

"You're right. It's not fair that you're so beautiful and so sexy."

As though to prove his point, his hands skimmed her shoulders and down her back, cupping her rear and lifting her. Instinctively, she wrapped her legs around his waist, locking herself where his arousal nudged between her thighs.

"I thought cold water was supposed to lower a man's ardor," she teased.

"It'd take an iceberg to cool me off around you, Mischief." His legs scissored to keep their heads above water.

The tantalizing motion of his body moving intimately against hers set her pulse beating ever more rapidly where flesh met flesh. Framing his rugged face between her hands, she kissed him. Her tongue toyed with his in a dance meant to be mimicked by another part of their bodies. Slowly she felt them sinking beneath the surface again, and it didn't matter if she drowned. She knew, however many years she might live beyond this moment, she would never find a greater happiness. Silence beat in her ears with a cadence that spoke of eternity.

With a powerful sweep of his legs, he sent them upward again. Almost reluctantly she drew a breath.

He gasped for air, too. "I think we'd better get onto land before we turn ourselves into food for the fish."

Her eyes widened in surprise. "There are fish in here?"

"A few. Nothing as big as a shark, of course."

She punched him on the shoulder, though the water blunted the blow. "I do not wish to be fish food, thank you very much."

"Fine by me." Still holding her, he sidestroked toward the edge of the pool, where a narrow, sandy beach allowed an easy exit. "I figure we're better off to finish what we've started on the blanket, anyway."

She had no desire to argue with his decision, particularly when he lifted her in his arms to carry her. Despite the warm air, gooseflesh covered her body. Water dripped from his hair onto her face, and she closed her eyes against the drops, against the thrill of anticipation.

Within moments of his laying her on the blanket, his caresses had begun to chase the chills away. When he rose above her, his head blocked the sun as it shimmered between the leaves overhead, and the cloudless sky vanished from view. Only Cord existed in her vision and in her heart as he entered her.

He made love to her leisurely, as though their first time together had taught him all those things that aroused her the most. The erotic feel of his tongue circling her ear. Sensual kisses, his teeth nipping lightly on her lower lip, then soothing the tiny pain away. His work-roughened hands caressing her flesh everywhere. And all the while he moved inside her, filling her, becoming a part of her as she became a part of him.

Though she tried to hold it back, to make this moment last, the pressure built to unendurable heights. She moved beneath him, wanting all he had to give. With a sob, she called out his name. Her climax clenched around him, drawing him deeper. She watched as his own control exploded, and she welcomed him as he surged into her one last time.

INSECTS BUZZED NEARBY and the smell of wild grass mixed with the scent of sex. The creek made a rhythmic hissing sound as it slid past the bank and tumbled over the rock dam.

Lying on his back with Allie's head on his shoulder, Cord figured he didn't have enough strength to budge even to get out of the way of a stampede.

"You hungry yet?" he asked, hoping she wasn't.

"Umm." Her fingers teased at the hair on his chest, parting, then smoothing it flat. "Men have such interesting bodies. So different than women."

"I think that's part of the plan."

"A very clever plan."

The sun had moved. What used to be dappled shade where he'd laid their blanket was now in full sun. Allie's skin was warm to his touch.

"You'd better get your clothes back on or you'll burn," he warned. In contrast, he often worked without a shirt and his torso was well tanned. But the rest of his body was as pale as a baby's, as susceptible to the sun as Allie's.

"But I am so comfortable where I am, I hate to move."

Cord understood that, but he didn't want either of them to burn so badly they wouldn't be able to enjoy the activities he had in mind for this evening. His sister wasn't due back until tomorrow. They still had the house to themselves. He didn't want to waste a moment of the time they had together.

All too soon Allie would leave him. In his experience, that's what women did.

Sitting up, and bringing her with him, he reached for her blouse, helping her on with it.

"Spoilsport," she accused him, though the spark of mischief in her eyes carried no sting.

"You'll thank me later, I promise."

He was reaching for his own shirt when he heard a sound. Voices. Riders on horseback. On the other side of the hill.

He scrambled to get to his jeans. "Get your clothes on in a hurry. Someone's coming."

Hopping from one foot to another, he pulled on his pants. He didn't bother with his boots. Barefoot, he rushed up the hill, hoping to head off the unexpected visitors and give Allie time to get dressed. He reached the top and met two riders on sleek Arabian mounts— Nick Grayson and his bride, the former Jessica Coleman.

Splaying his fingers through his still damp hair, he

said, "You two back from your honeymoon already?"

"Hey, Cord, how are you?" Jessica reined in her mount. "Nick and I have to get back to Dallas for a merger meeting tomorrow, but we wanted to stop by the Desert Rose to say hello first." She eyed Cord suspiciously. "How is it a big-time Texas rancher like you has enough free time for skinny-dipping these days?"

Cord frowned, uncomfortable with Jessica's penetrating gaze. Her eyes—one green and one blue—had a way of seeing right through a person's secrets. "How is it you know about our swimming hole, anyway?" During his youth it had been a firm rule among the Coleman boys and himself that girls weren't welcome here.

Of course, Allie's presence today was the exception. It was *his* swimming hole, after all.

Nick hooked his knee over his saddle horn. "Jess told me all about how she used to sneak over here to watch you and her cousins go swimming."

Heat rose to Cord's cheeks. "You watched us?"

"A girl has to learn about boys somehow." She didn't appear at all remorseful about her snooping. "Besides, as soon as Alex said I couldn't come along, I knew I'd move heaven and earth to find out what you guys were up to. Which wasn't all that impressive, by the way."

Embarrassed, Cord sputtered, "Geez, Jess, give a guy a break, huh?"

"We were thinking of giving the swimming hole a try ourselves."

"Uh, I'm not sure that's a good idea."

Jessica's gaze shifted to a spot behind him. "Uh-oh, looks like we interrupted something, Nick."

Cord glanced over his shoulder at Allie, who was walking up the hill toward him. "I was just showing my, er, housekeeper around the ranch. We were, uh, having a picnic."

Jessica's eyebrows shot up, and Nick visibly stifled a laugh.

"Right," Nick said, grinning. "I was planning to show Jess something, too."

"Same thing he's been showing me for the past couple of weeks, I'd venture." Love filled the look Jessica shared with her groom. They'd known each other a long time, and it appeared they'd finally stopped arguing long enough to discover they were meant for each other. "Mind you, I've enjoyed every minute of his show-and-tell, but we don't have to butt in on your picnic."

"No, that's okay. No problem." He reached out a hand to Allie, who managed to look more at ease than he felt. Her shirt was tucked in, her hair pulled back and held with a silver clasp. "Jessica and Nick Grayson, I'd like you to meet, ah, Leila Khautori. She's filling in while Maria is helping her daughter with a new baby."

Nick tipped his Stetson, a fancy beige one worn by urban cowboys, not working ranch hands, although he knew his way around horses about as well as any member of the Coleman clan did. "Nice to meet you."

Jessica said a friendly hello. "I'm glad Cord found someone to help out. I guess Brianna's been pretty busy handling the ranch bookkeeping, right?"

"Yeah, right," Cord mumbled. "She's up in New Hampshire right now. She'll be back tomorrow."

Jessica's look was all too knowing.

Allie stepped forward. "I am sure Cord would like you to join us for our picnic. There is more than enough for you both."

"That's all right." With a flick of her hand, Jessica waved off the invitation. "There's another spot down by the lake we can explore. It's a big country. You two enjoy yourselves here."

"Take care." Nick touched the brim of his hat again and slipped his feet back into the stirrups.

"Don't be strangers, you hear?" Cord said. "Jess, I know your mother would miss you if you didn't come around often enough."

With another wave, the two of them turned their horses downstream toward the lake that the creek flowed into.

Allie waited until they were out of sight before she spoke. "They know what we were doing, don't they?"

"Probably. It wouldn't be too hard to guess."

"Will they tell the Colemans?"

"Maybe not. Jessica pretty well knows when to keep her mouth shut."

"If she does tell them, what will they think of me?" Allie's eyes were sad and troubled.

Cord cursed himself. By not keeping his pants zipped and his hands off of Allie, he'd put her in an awkward position. The princess of Munir would be expected to remain above reproach. In addition to taking her virginity, he'd jeopardized her reputation. Not to mention he'd compromised himself, knowing she was engaged to another man.

Hell, he'd made a mess of things. He didn't how to undo it.

And he didn't know how to stop wanting her.

Sighing with worry, Allie turned to walk back down the hill to their picnic blanket. If Jessica or Nick mentioned the encounter to the Colemans, they might start asking questions—questions she wasn't prepared to answer.

The outcome of her adventure at the Flying Ace was inevitable. She'd known that from the start. But she hadn't expected the reality of leaving to hurt so much.

Tears pressed at the back of her eyes as she waited for Cord to join her beside the blanket.

"When I arrived at your ranch, you asked me what I did in service to my mistress. This evening it will be my pleasure to show you."

CORD CLENCHED HIS TEETH. She was driving him crazy.

After a light supper, Allie had filled the big tub in the master bathroom with water and sprinkled in about ten times more bubble bath than was called for. Then she'd bathed him like he was a baby. Except his reactions hadn't been at all childlike.

Now she had him sprawled across the king-size bed while she oiled his body, the scent reminding him of exotic places and romantic Arabian nights. Her hands touched him everywhere. Kneading his back and shoulders. Massaging his buttocks. Skimming down his thighs. With the sides of her hands, she pummeled his calf muscles. Even his feet and toes earned her careful attention.

He teetered on the sweet edge between pain and pleasure.

And she refused to let him touch her in return.

Cord groaned. "You're killing me, Mischief." With his face buried in the pillow, his words were muffled.

"Oh, I hope not, master." She began working her way back up his legs. "I have more plans for you when I have finished with this."

"Are you telling me this is what a lady-in-waiting does for her mistress?"

"Well, perhaps not exactly the same. I don't recall this." She kneaded his buttocks, then slid her hand between his legs.

His body jerked in response. "God, I hope not."

"Or this." She followed the path of his spine with her lips and tongue, leaving of trail of sexual heat that burned his entire body. "Is that something that pleases you?"

"Oh, yeah." A moan of pleasure escaped his lips.

"Perhaps if I start again and this time proceed more slowly—"

In a quick movement, he flipped onto his back, pulling Allie up to straddle him. "As of right now, you're done with show-and-tell, sweetheart. It's time for me to take control of the situation before I explode."

Which was exactly what he did minutes later, in the most deeply satisfying climax he'd ever experienced.

THE NEXT DAY, Brianna hefted her suitcase from the luggage carousel at the Austin airport. The strain of settling the final details of her aunt's estate hadn't been as difficult as she had feared. New Hampshire and her life there was behind her now. She'd come home to Texas.

Smiling to herself, she pulled her suitcase through the automatic doors and stepped out into the heat of midday.

At the curb a man in a white robe was arguing loudly with a limo driver, who was peering dejectedly under the hood of his vehicle. With a second look, Brianna recognized the angry gentleman as Sheikh Ashraf Bahram, an associate of the Coleman family. Rafe, she recalled.

Although she was tempted to ignore the situation, basic good manners demanded she offer her help. Be neighborly.

"Excuse me. Sheikh Bahram?"

His head whipped around, his eyes narrowing on her in a way meant to intimidate. "Yes. What is it?"

She'd spent most of her life as a shy wallflower, unable to stick up for herself. But no longer. She'd put that part of her life behind her along with the difficult memories of New Hampshire.

"I'm Brianna Taylor from the Flying Ace Ranch. If you're on your way to the Desert Rose, I'd be happy to give you a lift." She wasn't about to let this man intimidate her. He didn't, however, look all that pleased with her offer.

He set his jaw. "I'm not going to the Desert Rose. I'm going to the Flying Ace to retrieve my sister and take her back to Munir where she belongs."

A sudden understanding confirmed Brianna's earlier suspicions. Leila wasn't a servant at all, but a princess in disguise.

Brianna wondered how Cord would react to that revelation.

And *she* wouldn't miss being an eyewitness to Rafe's breaking the news for anything.

"Like I said, I'd be happy to give you a lift."

Chapter Eleven

Allie carried the hamper filled with dirty clothes into the laundry room. One thing she had learned during her stay at the Flying Ace was to take care of her own needs, elementary things like washing her clothes and cleaning up after herself. It made her more respectful of the work servants did—and ashamed of her own careless disregard for their feelings.

Returning to the kitchen, she slid the basket of eggs she'd gathered that morning into the refrigerator. The rooster had been particularly pesky, underfoot as she gently disturbed his hens to get at their eggs. Perhaps he was getting too old for his job as head rooster. But surely retirement rather than death by ax was a viable option.

Feeling domestic, Allie decided to try her hand at making baklava to celebrate Brianna's return home. The flaky pastry would appeal to Cord's sweet tooth.

Mittens jumped up onto the counter to bat at an ivy plant sitting on the windowsill. Allie snared her before she could knock over the clay pot.

''Be careful, Mittens, or I will have to rename you Trouble.''

Glancing outside, she saw Brianna's car arrive. A tail of dust settled back to the ground as she parked and got out of the car.

A guilty sense of regret pricked Allie's conscience. She liked Cord's sister, but Allie was sorry she and Cord would no longer have the house to themselves.

And then, to her surprise, the passenger door opened and a tall man in a flowing white robe exited the vehicle. Allie recognized him immediately.

Her brother!

Panic ripped through her. Where could she run? Where could she hide?

In the sweet name of Constantine, she didn't want to go back to Munir!

FROM THE BARN, Cord saw the sheikh get out of Brianna's car, and his stomach knotted in resignation. He'd known Allie's brother would show up eventually. But he hated that the moment had come. And he wished to God Allie had been honest with him before her brother showed up. She should have told him the truth…

He stuffed his hands into his pockets and walked with measured steps toward Sheikh Ashraf Bahram. Putting aside Allie's dishonesty for the moment, Cord had some serious questions that needed answers before he let her go anywhere with her brother.

With a glance at Brianna, who remained by the car,

watching the proceedings with avid interest, Cord nodded to the sheikh.

"I have come for my sister."

Cord could have dissembled, acted as though he didn't know what the sheikh was talking about. That wasn't Cord's way. "Took you a long time to miss her."

A hint of color tinged the sheikh's olive complexion. "My responsibilities have kept me busy recently. It only came to my attention yesterday that Allie had not returned to Munir with me."

"You and your sister are real close, huh?" So close he was planning to marry Allie off to some guy who scared her—or worse. That didn't sound like brotherly love to Cord.

"Mr. Brannigan." Apparently not interested in answering Cord's questions, the sheikh narrowed his gaze. "If my sister is still here, I would like to speak with her. And I am hoping you have been a man of honor in your treatment of the princess."

The sheikh had Cord there. He hadn't been honorable toward Allie. He'd taken her virginity with little thought of the consequences she might suffer, and had done it knowing damn well she was supposed to marry another man.

Coming around to the front of the car, Brianna spoke up. "If she's inside, I can go find her."

Shaking his head, Cord waved off Brianna's offer. "Let's all go inside. We've got some talking to do before anyone goes anywhere."

He walked up the porch steps and opened the heavy

wooden front door. The sheikh went inside, his back as straight as a soldier's, his head held at the same regal angle Allie often employed when making a point—like when she'd insisted the fool rooster shouldn't be beheaded.

Brianna followed him into the cool house. "Cord, before you do anything rash—"

"Entertain the sheikh for a couple of minutes, okay? I need to talk to Allie alone first."

"Don't yell at her," Brianna warned. "She must have had a good reason to do what she did."

Cord scowled. "I never yell at anyone." He didn't intend to now. But he did plan to get at the truth, one way or another.

He found Allie in the kitchen holding her kitten, her face as pale as a November moon, her dark eyes round with dread, and he felt another punch in the gut. Why the hell hadn't she told him the truth long before now? He wanted to grab her, shake the truth out of her.

Kiss her.

Instead he kept his hands to himself, which was what he should have done in the first place. "Your brother's here."

She moistened her lips with her tongue, pressed them together. "Yes, I saw him."

"You want to tell me why you decided to play at being a housekeeper? Was it just a lark to see if you could fool some dumb Texas cowboy?"

She gasped at his accusation. "Oh, no, never that. Please believe me." She lowered Mittens to the floor and the kitten scampered off. "I only wanted to stay in America for a while. Women are so free and independent here. I wanted to taste a little of that freedom before I was forced to marry Sardar Bin Douri." She lowered her gaze.

"You never intended to stay in Texas?" That's what Cord had assumed all along. He just hated to hear it from Allie, and felt doubly the fool for having forgotten his vow to keep his hands off of her.

"I'm sorry I didn't tell you the truth sooner. I wanted to—"

"Are you afraid of this Bin Douri guy?"

"A little."

"Did you tell your brother how you feel? That you're scared of the man he wants you to marry?"

"He would only tell me not to listen to gossip, that Bin Douri is his business associate and would never harm me."

"But he has hair growing out his ears."

She nodded, her eyes sheened with tears. "I don't want to go back to Munir."

Cord was torn with indecision. He'd vowed to keep his emotions out of the mix. Getting involved in a family dispute would put him in the middle. Arranged marriages were apparently the norm where Allie came from. Who was he to argue against that?

Except, perversely, he didn't want her to go back to Munir any more than she wanted to go. And the image of her making love with another man—any other man—made bile rise in his throat. But how could he stop that from happening?

''Let's go talk to your brother.''

She drew a deep, melancholy breath that raised her breasts. At the moment, wearing a red strappy T-shirt and jeans, her long hair a loose fall of brown silk, she looked nothing like the haughty princess who had arrived at the Flying Ace less than two weeks ago. In that time, she'd learned to cook—sort of. She'd cleaned a chicken coop—mostly—and had washed windows and scrubbed floors.

And made love with so much passion, Cord couldn't imagine any other woman satisfying him as completely as she did.

Desperately, he wanted to assure her she wouldn't have to do anything she didn't want to do. That everything would be all right. But what could he say when her brother was in the living room, ready to pack her off to Munir and into the arms of another man?

A man Cord was beginning to hate.

GATHERING HERSELF, Allie lifted her chin. It was time to face her brother. Surely she could explain to Rafe that she was no longer willing to marry a man she did not love. It didn't even matter that Bin Douri might have killed his wife.

Now that Cord had taught her of love, she would never settle for less.

Holding her head high, she walked past Cord, out of the kitchen and into the living room. Both Rafe and Brianna stood as she entered.

"I want you to pack your bag, Aliah. Our plane is waiting for us at the airport."

"Wait a minute, Your Highness," Brianna interrupted. "Don't you think you ought to at least hear your sister's side of the story?"

"She knows what she has done will bring shame on the family name if the news spreads in our country. If she doesn't return to marry Sardar Bin Douri, those who oppose our rule will—"

"I'm not going back with you." Allie's knees trembled as she defied both her brother and the ancient traditions of her country. Though she had often been rebellious in childish ways and chafed under the restrictions of her life, this time she intended to stand her ground even if she had to appeal to the American government for asylum. *She would not return to Munir.*

"That's right, Sheikh." Cord stepped forward to stand beside her. "Allie's not going back to Munir."

Rafe's expression darkened, and Brianna gasped in surprise.

A seed of hope blossomed somewhere near Allie's heart, and she looked up at Cord. "I'm not?"

Cord didn't look at her. "I'm afraid I have a confession to make. Instead of acting honorably with your sister, Princess Aliah, I took advantage of her innocence."

"You didn't take advantage. I wanted you to—"

"Even though I knew she was a princess and engaged to another man, I seduced her. More than once."

"Cord!" Brianna said in a shocked tone.

Allie's face flushed as hot as the desert sun. He didn't have to tell her brother all the details! But more importantly...*he'd known?*

"Wait a minute! You *knew* I was a princess? When did you learn that?"

"It wasn't all that hard to figure out, Mischief. You're not exactly like any housekeeper I've ever met."

"Then you knew from the beginning?"

"Pretty darn close."

"And you—you *ordered* me to clean your foul chicken coop?" The sense of betrayal was so keen it was like a knife slicing through her heart. He'd *known,* yet he'd treated her as a...a *servant!* Never mind that she'd started the deception, hadn't been truthful herself.

"You could have said no. I expected you to."

She stumbled back a step as though she'd been slapped. She'd been so proud of all she'd done, of all she'd learned. And he had expected her to fail. To give up. He'd been toying with her all along.

Was that true of his lovemaking, too? she wondered frantically. Had it all been some cruel game to prove he could seduce a princess? A royal notch on his bedpost?

"None of this matters," Rafe interrupted. "I have pledged my word that Allie will marry—"

"Unless I miss my guess," Cord interrupted, "your guy is looking for a virgin, right? And sure as hell, he's not interested in a woman who might already be pregnant with my baby.''

The whole room went as silent as a stone. Only the tapping of Mittens's tiny claws on the hardwood floor as she tiptoed through the room broke the stillness.

Blood rushing through Allie's brain echoed in her head. She hadn't considered that possibility. *Cord's child!* A baby for her to hold and love might already be growing in her womb. All the more reason for her not to return to Munir.

"So I think the answer is obvious." Cord learned his hip against the back of an upholstered chair. "Allie and I are going to get married."

Her head snapped around and she glared at him. He'd spoken no words of love. He hadn't even *asked* her if she would be willing to share his life. He was worse than her brother and twice as bossy.

"Never!" Allie said in a harsh whisper. "I would rather walk barefoot on hot coals than live a life dominated by an overbearing man like you."

Whirling, she raced back to the kitchen and out the side door. She didn't know where she was going, could barely see through her tears. But she knew she could never return to Munir, nor could she marry a man who had betrayed her so heartlessly.

She loved Cord, and he had abused that love, throwing it in her face as though it counted for nothing.

CORD STOOD ROOTED in the living room, stunned by Allie's fury. He'd proposed, for God's sake. What more could a woman ask for? He was trying to save her reputation. To make things right.

"I've gotta go talk to Allie," he mumbled.

"No, I'll go after her," Rafe insisted. "She's my sister, and you've already done enough damage."

"Wait a minute!" Brianna stepped forward to block their path. "You guys just don't get it, do you?"

"What are you talking about? I proposed, didn't I?"

"With about as much romance as kicking her in the teeth."

In confusion, Cord frowned at his sister. "Romance? What's that got to do with anything? She doesn't want to go back to Munir. It's as simple as that. She can live here as my wife."

Brianna shook her head in obvious disapproval. "You two stay right where you are. *I'll* go talk to Allie. But I won't guarantee I can fix the mess you've created. If I were her, I'd be on the next flight to Timbuktu just to get away from the both of you."

As his sister left the room, Cord glared at the sheikh and Rafe glowered back at him.

Cord didn't know what the hell he'd done wrong, but he had the awful feeling Brianna was right. He'd tried to keep his emotions at bay and it had cost him more than he was willing to admit.

THE MARE WOULDN'T STAND still. Why in the name of heaven hadn't she learned to saddle a horse? She'd barely managed to bridle the animal without getting her thumb bitten off.

Eyes burning with tears of frustration and heartache, Allie hefted the heavy saddle again, this time landing it on the horse's back. Behind her, she heard footsteps entering the barn, which she ignored, reaching instead for the cinch to pull it tight. No matter what Cord said, she wasn't going to stay here. She was mortified by what he had told her brother, devastated by such a heartless proposal.

"You'll need a saddle blanket with that." Brianna stepped into the stall with her. "Let me help you."

Allie released a small sigh of relief that it was Brianna, not Cord, who'd followed her. Or perhaps it was disappointment, though she didn't wish to admit that even to herself. "I should know something as simple as how to saddle a horse."

"There's no way to know unless someone teaches you." Brianna removed the mare's saddle, set it aside and laid a blanket in its place on the horse's back. "Cord taught me shortly after I arrived here."

"He was more interested in having me learn to clean out chicken coops," Allie said with a trace of bitterness.

"I suspect he's realized his mistake by now." Expertly, Brianna settled the saddle in place, tossed the stirrup on top of it and grabbed the cinch from underneath. It all looked so easy. "Where are you planning to go?"

Brianna's question was so casual, it brought Allie up short, because she hadn't given the answer any thought. "I don't know. As far away from bossy, overbearing men as I can get."

"Why don't you go to the Desert Rose? I'm sure Vi Coleman will give you sanctuary until you decide what you want to do."

Instinctively, Allie stroked the mare's velvety nose. "What can I do? I don't really have any money of my own, only an allowance from Rafe." Which she generally overspent. "I don't know enough of anything to get a job, and I sincerely doubt anyone would be interested in hiring me as a housekeeper."

"Oh, I don't know. You could end up as curator at a Texas museum. You seem to have a flair for identifying historical records, and you did have some experience in Munir."

As much as Allie enjoyed antiquities, had relished her work at the museum in Munir as a welcome diversion from her royal routine, the prospect held little excitement for her at the moment.

Smiling, Brianna patted the horse's neck. "Why don't you worry about one thing at a time? Stay with Vi until the dust settles. By then, maybe one or both of those stubborn men will come to his senses."

"But I can't simply pop in on Mrs. Coleman and expect her to invite me to stay."

"Allie, Vi is the kindest woman I've ever met. She'll be thrilled to have you, I'm sure. She'll probably fawn all over you, pamper you and bake you some cookies. That's just the way she is."

"I no longer wish to be pampered." Vi Coleman had been a kind and gracious hostess when Allie and her brother had visited. And the fact was Allie had nowhere else to go. "My things—"

"I'll pack up for you and bring them over this afternoon, see how you're doing."

"You're sure it will be all right?"

"I'll even drive you over there and explain to Vi what's going on, if you'd like."

Allie considered that possibility. "No, it will be better if neither Cord nor my brother is aware you are helping me. I'd like them to not be entirely sure where I've gone."

"I don't know about Rafe, but I imagine Cord will track you down sooner rather than later." Her hand still resting on the horse's mane, Brianna studied Allie a moment. "If you don't mind me asking a personal question, are you in love with Cord?"

Guilty heat rushed to Allie's face. "It would not matter if I were or not. I will not under any circumstances marry a man who does not love me in return. Your brother has no such feelings for me."

"I wouldn't be too sure about that. But I do know Cord was hurt once by a woman and has been wary of love since then. He'll get himself sorted out— eventually."

"By then I may no longer be here." Allie's brother might take her away by force. Or she might find a way to leave on her own—become a museum worker. Or, more likely, a professional chicken-coop cleaner. In either case, Cord's change of heart—if he had one—would come too late.

Brianna gave her a quick hug. "If I've learned anything about my brother in this past year, it's that he can be a very determined man. I rather doubt you'll be staying long at the Desert Rose.''

Brianna stepped out of the stall, and Allie led the horse out, too. Placing her foot in the stirrup, she mounted. She was far less confident than Brianna that Cord would follow her. He had made the offer of marriage out of a guilty conscience for what he had done. By refusing his proposal she had relieved him of further responsibility. Surely he would leave it at that.

Which meant she would only have to deal with her brother—no easy task, she admitted, but one she had managed often enough to be confident of gaining her way.

She would stay in America—without Cord's help.

CORD WASN'T ABOUT TO SIT down unless Rafe did, so they both paced the room, shooting daggers at each other with their eyes, waiting for Brianna to return with Allie.

She could be pregnant with my child.

Cord cursed himself under his breath. He could chalk up another of his lapses into stupidity. He'd remembered to use a condom the first time. After that he'd wanted Allie so badly, he hadn't given protection a thought, almost as if at some subliminal level he'd actually hoped he'd get her pregnant.

As if she'd want to have my babies.

He and Rafe paced past each other, their shoulders brushing because neither of them would give an inch.

"In my country I could have you shot for what you have done," Rafe said.

"I wouldn't try that in Texas. Your sister's a consenting adult."

"She's naive. Inexperienced. An innocent."

"And you were going to marry her off to some guy who'd killed his first wife."

"What?" Halting abruptly, Rafe spun around and marched back to Cord. "Where on earth did you get that idea?"

"From Allie. She's scared to death of the man."

"What nonsense. Sardar is almost like an uncle to me. He didn't kill his wife—he would not be capable of such a thing. The poor woman had a congenital heart condition. He was devastated when she died."

"You're sure?"

"Of course I'm sure. And when Sardar recovered from his loss, he thought to take Allie as his wife. He has always been fond of my sister and knew she would make a good mother to his young daughters. Anything else she may have heard was no more than the idle gossip of women who have nothing better to do with their days."

There was enough sincerity in Rafe's eyes to make Cord believe him. "But Allie and this Sardar don't love each other? He's older and he's got—" Cord wasn't going to tell Rafe the biggest problem was hair growing out of Allie's fiancé's ears. Hell, a pair of scissors could solve that problem. Cord wasn't sure he wanted it fixed.

"It would be a good arrangement for both of our

families. Love and affection would no doubt come later.''

''Doesn't sound to me like Allie's going to agree to the marriage at all.''

Sitting down heavily on the couch, Rafe ran his fingers through his hair, which was several shades darker than Allie's, almost jet-black. Even so, there was a family resemblance between the siblings, their features equally dramatic.

''If my sister was afraid of Sardar, why didn't she tell me? Say something? I could have reassured her.''

The sheikh looked so worried now, Cord could almost sympathize with him. It couldn't be easy to be responsible for a younger sister. ''Maybe you're not around enough for her to confide in you. From what you said earlier, I gather you get pretty busy with your royal duties.''

''Evidently I've neglected my responsibilities to my sister.''

''And I took advantage of her. We're a hell of a pair, aren't we?''

Rafe glanced up with a hint of a smile. ''I'd say we're both at the mercy of women no matter what we do.''

Cord started to laugh at the same moment Brianna came in through the back of the house, dragging the suitcase she'd taken to New Hampshire behind her.

''Where's Allie?'' Cord asked when he saw that his sister was alone.

''Gone.''

He stared at her stupidly. ''Gone? Where?''

"I have no idea." She kept walking past him toward the bedroom wing of the house.

Rafe was on his feet. "Surely she told someone where she was going. One of the ranch hands, perhaps?"

"There wasn't anyone around that I saw."

"They're out checking fences." Which was what Cord had asked them to do this morning. "Did she take one of the cars?" Or worse yet, a five-gear truck she didn't know how to drive. Damn, if she'd done that, she could get herself killed.

"My car's still here. I don't know about the rest." Brianna vanished down the hallway with Mittens bounding after her, attacking a loose strap that was dangling from the suitcase.

"Well, hell!" Cord muttered.

"We have to find her," Rafe said.

"I know that. She can't have gone far, not if she's on foot." But the Flying Ace was a big ranch with lots of hazards that could cause trouble for a greenhorn—like stepping into a prairie dog hole and breaking her leg. Or having an up close and personal meeting with a testy bull. Or just plain getting lost.

The situation became even more troubling an hour later when Cord finally discovered she'd managed to saddle the quarter horse she'd ridden yesterday to the swimming hole.

"Can we track her?" Rafe asked as he looked out across the rolling landscape. Above the first row of trees, two hawks made lazy circles in an updraft while keeping their eyes on the ground in search of a mid-day meal.

"We?"

His expression narrowed with concern. "She's my sister, Cord."

Cord nodded in understanding. "I'll round us up some horses."

Chapter Twelve

Allie arrived at the Desert Rose filled with a mixture of anxiety and heartache, and slightly out of breath. Glancing around in the hope that no one had noticed her, she dismounted near the back door, tethering the horse to a hitching post. Her heart beat hard and rapidly as she walked up the steps to the porch. What would she do if Vi Coleman turned her away?

She'd never in her life gone begging for a place to stay.

She didn't want to return to Munir.

And she desperately didn't want to face Cord again after his cold, unfeeling proposal.

Why couldn't he love her as deeply as she loved him?

Her hand trembled as she knocked on the door.

The wait seemed interminable before Vi responded to the knock. The older woman stood in the open doorway, a puzzled expression on her face and no hint of recognition. "Yes?"

"Mrs. Coleman, I'm Allie Bahram. Sheikh Rafe's sister."

"Land sakes! I didn't recognize you, Princess." Taking in Allie's casual jeans and top with a quick glance, Vi looked past Allie toward the horse barns. "Did your brother come back to check on the mare?"

"Not exactly. I am very sorry to bother you and to come to your home unannounced, but I need your help."

"My help? Come in, my dear. I'll certainly do whatever I can for you." Opening the door wide, Vi stepped back. As though she were as anxious as Allie, her hand went to her hair, smoothing fine strands of red touched with a few threads of gray. "You'll have to forgive the mess. I wasn't expecting company."

"Please do not apologize. It is I who have inconvenienced you."

Vi laughed a little nervously. "Well, it's not every day a princess shows up at my back door."

Allie paused in the middle of the kitchen. From the scent of spices filling the air, the presence of knick-knacks on the cluttered counter and baby photos held with magnets on the refrigerator door, she could tell this was a room filled with love. Brianna had been right. Vi Coleman was the kind of woman who would help her.

"Mrs. Coleman, I am hoping to remain in America indefinitely, which means I will no longer be a princess."

Saying the words out loud made Allie fully realize what her decision meant. Her pampered life as a member of a royal household would be behind her forever. In America she would have to make her own way, with her wits or whatever other strengths she had.

She smiled at the thought, sensing she was about to embark on yet another new adventure. From this one there would be no turning back. "Please call me Allie."

"Then you must call me Vi." the older woman pulled out a chair at the kitchen table. "Sit down here. I'll get you a cup of coffee, or tea if you prefer, and you can tell me what's troubling you."

"Coffee would be very nice."

Gratefully, Allie took a seat. When Vi had poured coffee for them both, she sat down, too, nodding that she was ready to listen.

Taking a deep breath, Allie began. She told Vi how she had disguised herself as Leila and pretended to be a housekeeper for Cord, how it had begun as a small rebellion—a way to avoid for a short time an unwelcome arranged marriage—and had grown into something else. She gave scant details about her relationship with Cord, but Allie knew from Vi's expression that the woman was far too perceptive to ignore the implications of Cord's proposal.

"So you turned Cord down," Vi said as Allie finished her tale.

"I had to." She fingered the flower design on her empty cup. "He does not love me."

"And what is it you would like me to do?"

Allie glanced up into Vi's understanding eyes. "If it is not too much trouble, I would like to stay here for a few days. I'm hoping I can find a job. Perhaps as a housekeeper until I can make arrangements for permanent status in your country.''

''That might be possible, I suppose.'' Pensively, Vi got up and brought the coffeepot back to the table. ''The fact is, all three of my nephews' wives could use a baby-sitter these days more than a housekeeper. They'd love to be able to get a few hours of peace and quiet now and then.''

''I can do that! I love babies. Do you think they would hire me? I could be like a nanny for all the babies.'' In her excitement, Allie spoke rapidly, her voice rising in pitch. She'd never expected to make a living on her own by cuddling babies. It seemed a perfect solution to her problems. Much better than scrubbing floors and other such onerous tasks.

Vi's hand covered hers. ''Why don't you plan to stay here with me for a few days until you can make other arrangements? The house is dreadfully empty these days with just my husband and myself living here. We'd love to have you for company. Meanwhile, we can talk to Hannah, Rena and Abbie. I'm sure they'll be thrilled with the idea of having a regular baby-sitter nearby.''

''Thank you, Mrs. Coleman—Vi. Brianna said you'd be able to help me.'' Allie had no doubt that Vi, a doting grandmother, volunteered as a baby-sitter when she could. But in the Coleman family there were plenty of babies who needed attention.

THERE WERE TOO DAMN MANY horse tracks around a working ranch to make picking up Allie's trail easy.

It took Cord hours and a good many false starts to realize she'd headed for the Desert Rose. By then, both he and Rafe were hot, tired and cranky from being worried sick that Allie might have gotten herself in trouble, and they rode hell-bent for the neighboring horse ranch—which was a good two miles away riding cross-country.

Cord spotted Allie's mount tied up behind the main house near a watering trough, the saddle on the porch. "There's the horse she was riding."

"Allie has always been a little impulsive, but running away like this—" Rafe leaped off his horse and bounded up the steps, using his fist to pound on the door "—this time she has gone too far."

No happier about the situation than Allie's brother, Cord was right behind him. He was about to open the door himself and go on inside, as he often had as a kid, when Vi appeared.

"Hello, Cord," she said in her usual calm manner. "Sheikh Bahram, it's good to see you again."

"I believe my sister is here. I wish to see her."

"I'm not at all sure she wants to see you—certainly not if you're going to use that tone with her."

Rafe sputtered, and Cord stepped forward. "Look, Vi, we need to talk with Allie. She's got things all wrong."

"Has she? You two bullies come busting in here like you own the place—"

"I didn't bust," Cord protested.

"I assure you, Mrs. Coleman, I have my sister's best interests at heart. I don't, of course, know what she has told you, but she's being a very foolish girl. If she doesn't return to Munir with me, allow me to work out any problems she may have with the marriage I have arranged, she will be throwing away her whole life."

Vi raised her brows, looking at Cord in a way that made him squirm. "Is that what you think, too?"

"She can stay here if she wants to. I've offered to marry her."

"So she told me. Very generous of you, I'm sure."

Feeling like a kid who'd been caught tipping over an outhouse with someone inside, Cord yanked off his hat. "Vi, I need to talk to Allie. Now, I can wait out here till she comes out—and she can't stay in the house forever. Or you can let me in."

"I will talk with her as well," Rafe insisted.

"Very well." Vi held up her hand when they both started to crowd forward. "You two young men listen to me and listen well. Allie Bahram is a guest in my home. I will not have you berate or bully her while she is under my roof. And I suggest you both remember that she is of age and has every right to make up her own mind about where she will live and with whom. Do you understand me?"

"Yes, ma'am," Cord said automatically. This wasn't the first time Vi Coleman had called him on the carpet about some stunt he'd pulled, although it had been a long time since she'd given him such a tongue-lashing.

Apparently unused to taking orders from anyone,

particularly a woman, Rafe gave a reluctant nod of agreement.

Cord went inside ahead of Rafe, and when he spotted Allie standing in the kitchen, his breath caught in his lungs, both in relief and in admiration. Despite her American clothes, she looked as regal as he had ever seen her—head held high, shoulders back, hands folded quietly at her slender waist. From her solemn expression, he couldn't tell whether she was expecting to meet her subjects or her executioner. Or which role she had cast him to play.

Rafe brushed past him. "Why didn't you tell me you had heard that ridiculous rumor about Sardar?"

She lifted her chin another notch. "Because you would have told me it was a ridiculous rumor, assuming you had listened to me at all."

"I'm sorry, Allie, I really am." Rafe lifted his shoulders in a helpless gesture. "I haven't meant to ignore you or your concerns. Come back to Munir where you belong. I promise I'll talk with Sardar. I will allow you time to get to know him better and ease your fears."

"I am not going to marry him, Rafe. I won't do it."

"Why on earth not?" Rafe's question came out sharply.

"Because I do not love him and never could."

"You can't stay in America much longer, Sister. Your visa will run out soon. You don't have a job, much less any job skills. You have no money of your own. You must come home with me and we will work things out with Sardar. I promise I won't force you to marry him if you decide you do not want to.''

Allie's gaze swung purposefully to Cord.

He knew what Allie wanted, but he couldn't give it to her. After his experience with Sandra—her running away with a married man virtually at the moment he had planned to propose—he wasn't sure he was capable of love. More importantly, he'd learned that love in all its various forms created more problems than it solved, and hurt like hell, too.

''She can stay in America as long as she likes, as my wife,'' Cord said.

Pain flashed in Allie's eyes an instant before she shuttered her reaction. ''With Vi's assistance, I have arranged employment for myself. I do not need you.'' She glanced at her brother. ''Either of you.''

''You've what?'' Cord and Rafe said in unison.

Stepping forward, Vi wrapped an arm around Allie's shoulders. ''Allie is going to be the Coleman nanny, helping out all three of my nephews' wives. For now, she'll be staying here with me. Randy and I will help her to get a permanent visa, and then she'll be free to come and go as she pleases and work anywhere she likes.''

''Dammit, Vi—''

''Don't you swear at me, Cord Brannigan. I still know how to make a good sturdy switch, and don't think I'd be afraid to use it on you just because you're bigger than I am, either.''

It was an idle threat, Cord knew, but he didn't want to tempt Vi. So far as he could recall, she'd never whipped any of the children she'd raised—including the kid from the neighboring ranch who hadn't had a mother to keep him in line. But Vi looked just mad enough and sufficiently protective of Allie to make good on her promise if he pressed his luck. He was a lot smarter than that.

He backed up a step just as the back door opened and Cade Coleman came inside.

"Hey, Vi, there're a bunch of Flying Ace horses outside." Discovering Cord, Rafe and Allie in the kitchen, he halted abruptly. "Uh, what's going on?"

Rafe spoke up. "I had an unexpected opportunity to return to the States to take care of some family business. I thought as long as I was here, I would look in on Khalahari, see how the mare is doing."

Visibly perplexed by Rafe's unexpected appearance, Cade glanced at Allie and then nodded as though he'd figured out what was going on. "Right. Well, whenever you're ready, come on down to the horse barn. Khalahari's as healthy as a horse—if you'll excuse the expression—and her pregnancy seems to be coming along just fine."

"Now would be a good time," Vi said. "Cord will go with you." It was an order, not a suggestion.

Mashing his hat back on his head, Cord shot a final look at Allie. So she had a job of sorts and thought she could take care of herself.

That was fine by him. He could get on with the rest of his life, no strings attached. No emotional involvement. He had plenty to keep him busy at the Flying Ace. That was just how he liked it.

ALLIE SNARED eleven-month-old Sarah Coleman before she tumbled off a throw pillow on the floor she'd managed to climb onto.

Abbie, the baby's mother, who Allie had beaten to the rescue, laughed. "She's like a little monkey and climbs everything in sight, but she hasn't quite mastered the coming down part yet."

"She will soon learn." With ease, Allie distracted the baby by putting her on a rocking horse small enough that her feet touched the floor. The child rocked back and forth, making excited noises, apparently urging the horse to go faster.

After dinner, the informal living room at the Desert Rose had filled with women, their babies and an explosion of toys. Ella Grover, the Colemans' energetic cook and housekeeper, served ice cream and homemade cookies while the infants were shifted from one set of loving arms to another. One of Hannah's five-month-old twin boys currently resided in Vi's lap, while the other one tugged on his aunt Rena's long auburn hair. In turn, Rena's twin babies were being shared by Hannah and Brianna, the latter of whom had delivered Allie's suitcase earlier and stayed for dinner.

Jessica and Nick had left early that morning to return to Dallas or they no doubt would have joined the group, as well.

"So you just left Cord and Sheikh Rafe on their own for dinner?" Rena asked Brianna.

"I'm sure Cord can manage to stir up something to eat. He's very self-reliant."

"I hope he doesn't ask my brother to cook," Allie commented. "They would both starve."

The women laughed, and Allie felt guilty that she had known as little about preparing meals as Rafe until she'd begun masquerading as a housekeeper.

"I've got four brothers," Abbie said, "and they barbecue great steaks and cook a mouthwatering omelette, but none of them ever learned how to put the seat down on the toilet."

Rena insisted the problem was genetic, and laughter erupted again.

Vi relinquished baby Ryan to Allie while she went to speak to Ella, and Allie sat in a comfortable chair, cuddling the sleepy baby. In some ways this evening was much like being in the women's quarters at the palace, with lots of feminine laughter and jokes at the expense of men they knew. But at a more subtle level this was quite different.

Here, Allie wasn't a princess. She was one of them. There was no deferring to her wishes, or false agreement with whatever outlandish thing she might say. Here she was an equal.

These warm American women had accepted her as a friend.

Because of her position and the infernal politics of royalty, she'd had few true friends in her life. Which made these women whom she had only recently met all the more important to her.

Young Sarah grew weary of the rocking horse, demanding attention from her mother, and Abbie lifted the child into her lap.

In a quiet moment, Rena said, "I think I can safely speak for all of us, Allie. We are delighted with the idea of you baby-sitting our brood of Coleman babies from time to time."

The other women nodded in agreement.

"It will be my honor and pleasure," Allie said.

"And as far as I am concerned," Rena continued, "you are doing the right thing by refusing an arranged marriage. I happen to have personal experience in that regard."

"As I remember the story," Abbie countered, grinning, "you *thought* Cade was Mac when you married him. Although I don't know how you could have thought that, since Mac is much more handsome than his *younger* brother."

"They're identical twins," Hannah protested. "How could either of them be more good-looking than the other? Particularly since my husband, Alex, as the eldest son, got all the good looks in the family, anyway."

The good-natured hoots of laughter coming from Rena and Abbie halted only when Vi reappeared.

"Sounds to me like I'm going to have to keep you girls separated if those precious babies are going to get any rest at all tonight."

"Speaking of which..." Hannah stood, signaling that it was time to shift the babies back to their mothers so they could all go home.

Reluctantly, Allie gave up baby Ryan to Hannah. "He is so dear. Call me anytime, please."

"My veterinarian business seems to be picking up,

so you may get more calls than you were counting on from me.''

''Impossible.'' Allie's only regret was that she did not have a baby of her own to hold after these children went home.

''Well, if you're sure...'' Hannah glanced around the room. ''I do need to make an early call at the Fitzsimmons place tomorrow. Alex was going to watch the twins for me, but he said something about wanting to go into Austin and he'd have to put that off unless—''

''I would love to care for Ryan and Justin if you need me.''

''Then it's a deal. Let's say seven o'clock.''

Allie was more than happy to agree to the early hour. Her first real job! Self-confidence surged through her, along with a sense of accomplishment.

''I'd better warn you, ladies.'' Brianna stood with the others. ''I'm not a mind reader, of course, but I suspect Cord may not be willing to leave the situation as it is for long. So if I were you, I'd take advantage of Allie's offer to baby-sit as soon as possible.''

The young mothers snapped their attention back to Allie.

Rena's gaze was the most perceptive of the lot. ''Is there something you haven't told us that we ought to know about you and Cord?''

Allie forced herself not to flinch. ''Nothing. Nothing at all.''

WHEN THE OTHERS HAD LEFT and Vi had retired for the night with her husband, Randy, Allie found herself in the guest room she had used to change in when she'd first visited the Desert Rose with her brother. Tasteful rosewood furniture filled the room, and there was a comfortable sitting area with two upholstered chairs by the French windows. A light silk spread in shades of burgundy covered the inviting bed, but Allie wasn't in the least sleepy. The day had brought too many changes.

Too many disappointments.

She stepped out onto the veranda into the warm night air. The moon illuminated the nearby lake and, along the top of a ridge, cast a row of trees in silver. Bats flitted in and out of the shadows between the ranch house and outbuildings. Beneath the veranda, crickets chirped from the flower beds, and the sweet smell of roses climbing up the trellis filled the air.

Allie sighed in dissatisfaction. From this vantage point she couldn't see the Flying Ace. That was where her heart belonged, except she didn't dare risk her heart in the hands of someone who couldn't love her.

That would be an even more foolish mistake than masquerading as a housekeeper.

Fighting back tears, she slid her hand across her belly, trying to sense the tiniest bit of life forming inside her womb.

If only...

AT THE FLYING ACE, Cord folded up the backgammon board and set it aside. Rafe was a lucky son of a gun, or maybe it was Cord's total inability to concentrate on the two games they'd played that had caused him to lose—big time.

It had made no sense to send Rafe into Bridle to stay the night at a motel, so Cord had invited him to remain at the ranch. He hadn't counted on Brianna ducking out, leaving him stuck handling the dinner. He'd fried up a couple of steaks and baked some potatoes. Nothing fancy, but neither he nor Rafe had been particularly hungry.

Brianna had come home later, going straight to her room with barely a howdy to either Rafe or Cord, as if she were mad at them both.

That made no sense. *He'd* tried to do the right thing.

So why the hell had Allie turned down his proposal?

Getting up from the table, Cord walked outside and stood in the middle of the patio near the fountain, trying to let the soft fall of water ease his tension while he looked up at the nearly full moon.

It wasn't that he was ugly as sin. He knew that much. And it wasn't that Allie didn't enjoy making love with him. No woman could have faked her passionate responses.

Granted, his proposal hadn't been the most romantic in the world, but under the circumstances she should have given him some slack. Dammit, her brother was about to drag her back to Munir. Cord had offered her an alternative.

So maybe he wasn't Prince Charming. Or a prince at all. But he could provide a woman with a good life. A comfortable life with most anything she needed or wanted.

Of course, it got too hot here in Texas during the summer. But Munir wasn't exactly frigid, either. Maybe a little less humid. And being a rancher's wife had never been easy.

Dammit all! He'd have to talk to Allie tomorrow—without her brother around. He was sure he could make her see reason.

She couldn't support herself by baby-sitting. Any day now her visa would run out and she'd be deported. Her best choice in order to avoid marrying Bin Douri was to marry Cord. As soon as possible.

That's exactly what he intended to explain to her first thing tomorrow morning.

BRIANNA SLIPPED INTO BED and pulled the sheet up over her. Mittens leaped onto the bed, mewling and pawing the pillow next to Brianna's head, lonely for Allie.

"Don't you worry, Mittens. Allie will be back soon, I'm sure."

As a child, Brianna had learned to keep her own counsel. In the past year, since she'd moved to the Flying Ace, she had grown fond of her brother, and believed he reciprocated the feeling. Eventually he'd ask her advice about Allie.

Certainly he wouldn't go to Allie's brother for guidance about love. The sheikh was far too arrogant.

Far too attractive in a foreign, exotic way, she admitted.

Cord would come to her when the time was right. Meanwhile, she'd bide her time, knowing exactly how her brother could touch Allie's heart—when he stopped being so mule-headed about falling in love.

Chapter Thirteen

The next morning Cord went to see Allie, to make her see reason. He found her walking along the short-cut path from the Desert Rose main house to the smaller guest house that Alex and Hannah had made their own, expanding it to provide quarters for Hannah's veterinarian business.

Cantering Jimmy Boy across the grassy field, he reined the horse to a walk, falling into step beside Allie. "Good morning."

She didn't look up, but kept on walking.

He persisted. "Beautiful morning, isn't it? Not too hot yet." When she didn't respond, he turned Jimmy Boy in front of her.

She gasped in surprise, putting her hands up to ward off the horse. Or more likely to keep Cord at a distance.

"Please do not bother me. I am on my way to work." She walked around him and his horse, continuing on the faint trail worn through the knee-high grass. Her fancy Stetson shaded her eyes and her jeans made swishing noises as she walked.

Cord dismounted and led his horse. "Work. That's great. Didn't think you'd get a job so soon."

She lifted her chin stubbornly. "I will be a very good baby-sitter."

"I don't doubt it for a minute. You're great with babies." More than once he'd seen how naturally loving Allie could be. "The problem is, you can't really support yourself by baby-sitting, not for the long haul. The job doesn't pay enough."

"Nannies are very well regarded in my country."

Grinding his teeth in frustration, he searched for a stronger argument to convince her she was being shortsighted. "Even if you can work for a while baby-sitting, eventually you'll have to go back to Munir. Is that what you want?"

"No."

He blocked her path again. They were halfway between the two houses, in a low spot where no one could see them, and Cord couldn't stand not touching Allie. Not showing her why she ought to stay in Texas—with him.

Catching her off guard, he dipped his head beneath the brim of her Stetson. He meant the kiss to surprise her. Persuade her. He gave it his best shot.

For a moment, she froze and then slowly relaxed, her innate passion responding to the slide of his tongue across the seam of her lips. When she opened for his penetration, Cord was sure he'd found the way to convince her. She couldn't be this susceptible to his kisses without wanting, at some level, to accept the offer he'd made. He only needed to work on that.

Coaxing her with his tongue, drawing her closer with his hand on her buttocks, he used all of his seductive powers to persuade her to yield to his will. He ignored the sting of guilt reminding him that he was taking advantage of an innocent woman. A woman who had been a virgin until he'd made love with her. But he would be good to her. He'd take an oath on it.

Marrying him was the best thing Allie could do.

When he broke the kiss, she looked up at him with dark, luminous eyes.

"Marry me, Allie." His voice rasped in his throat, more prayer than persuasion.

She licked her glistening lips. "Tell me why I should."

"You know why. You sure don't want to get stuck marrying that Bin Douri guy. You like it here in Texas and we're good together. Those seem like pretty darn good reasons to me."

She looked at him for a long while without speaking, her heart in her throat. She desperately wanted to accept his proposal. To spend her life loving Cord.

Marry me, Allie.

If she agreed, their marriage would be no more than a sham. An *arranged* marriage based on his bidding, not his love.

We're good together.

Even now her body betrayed her, revealing the desire she felt for Cord and would never feel for another man. Her blood sped hot and heavy through her veins;

her lips tingled from his kiss. But she wanted more. Her heart *demanded* more.

He stood silently waiting, watching her intently, expecting her to agree that marriage to him would be her wisest course. But when had she ever been wise? she mused with painful irony.

Somehow she found the strength to toss her head in regal disdain. "You are wrong, Cord Brannigan. What you say are not reasons to marry. That we are good together is why I took you for a lover. It is not why a woman selects a husband."

She forced herself to look directly into his green-gold eyes without letting her gaze slip to his lips—without recalling the taste of his lips on hers. Without remembering the feel of his hands caressing her. Without thinking of how he had filled her body, or her cries of pleasure and release.

Later she would deal with those memories. But not now. Not when her throat ached to tell him yes. Ached to agree to marry him under any terms he chose.

"Excuse me. I do not wish to be late for work."

Head held high, she edged past him, careful not to let her arm brush his, and walked up the rise toward Hannah Coleman's house and the twins she would care for.

CORD STOOD in stunned silence holding Jimmy Boy's reins, letting him graze on the rich grass of the Desert Rose, and watched Allie walk up the path.

He had been so sure she would marry him. The kiss had convinced him she wanted to.

But she wanted more than "good together."

She wanted more than he could offer, more than he had to give. He didn't have the courage to risk his heart again, risk emotions that made him vulnerable to a woman's rejection.

No man could be that strong.

When she vanished out of sight, he turned Jimmy Boy around and mounted. The thought of checking fences or moving cattle from one pasture to another held little appeal, but that's what he had to do.

If he was lucky, maybe keeping busy would help him forget how Allie felt in his arms and how he might never hold her again.

By the time Cord returned home, he was hot, tired and dirty. When he hung his hat on a peg on the service porch and walked into the kitchen, he half expected to see Allie there. Smiling at him. Her dark eyes flashing with amusement as she told him her refusal to marry him was only one of her mischievous tricks. All he had to do was name the day and they'd be married. She'd had enough of "working" for a living.

His wishful thinking burst like an overblown balloon when the only person in the kitchen was Rafe. And despite himself, Cord still couldn't stop from glancing around the room—just in case Allie was there.

"If you're looking for Brianna, she's not here,"

Rafe said as he expertly sliced a leftover roast beef. "She left a note saying she was having dinner in town with friends. That we should help ourselves to whatever was in the refrigerator."

"Great. At least we won't starve." Getting a glass from the cupboard, Cord ran some tap water and took a long drink to wash the dust from his throat—along with the gnawing sense of despair. "I think I'll ask Brianna to get in touch with Maria, my regular housekeeper. See when she's coming back."

"I went to see Allie today."

Cord swung around toward Rafe. "And?"

"She is a very stubborn woman."

Amen to that. "She's not going back to Munir with you?"

"She says not." Rafe plopped the sliced meat on a plate and got some bread from the yellow-and-red bread box on the counter. "I promised her I'd find another man for her to marry, one more to her taste. And still she did not relent."

"When she makes up her mind, she sure sticks to her guns."

"Evidently she has forgotten—or is determined to ignore—that arranged marriages are the norm in our culture. I myself will soon have to select a bride, and will ask my advisors to assist in making the appropriate arrangements." From the refrigerator Rafe took out a gallon of milk and poured himself a glass, carrying it to the table along with his plate. "Naturally, my bride will have a suitable background, just as Aliah's husband should have."

No doubt Cord didn't qualify, since nobody called him His Highness. *But she had called him master.* And to prove the point, he'd ordered her to do the dirtiest jobs on the ranch, all the while knowing she was a princess. He sure as hell hadn't treated her like one.

Surprise, surprise! She didn't want to marry him. Who could blame her?

Cord ran his fingers through his sweaty hair. "I've gotta go wash up before I eat."

He left Rafe slapping mayonnaise on his sandwich, and when he came back, Cord did the same for himself. They watched the news on TV and a preseason football game, then played backgammon again. This time Cord won, but it didn't make him feel any better.

He missed Allie too damn much.

How had she gotten so thoroughly under his skin in less than two weeks?

Maybe Allie's refusal of his proposal wasn't the only thing that didn't make sense.

Rafe called it a night, but Cord was too unsettled to think about sleep. Instead he went into the office, thinking he might do some work. The door to the storage room stood open, the mess Allie had made still there. Brianna hadn't even begun to straighten things out. Cord decided that would be a reasonable way to keep his mind occupied until he could sleep.

The papers as he sorted through them smelled musty, some so old they crackled in his hands. Allie had been right. There might be something worth keeping here—if not at the ranch, then at the university, for historical purposes.

The room was so cluttered with boxes and stacks of paper, it was hard to move around. Barely keeping his balance as he tiptoed past filing cabinets, he banged his ribs against an open drawer. He muttered a mild curse and tried to close it.

It wouldn't go. Pulling it open, he reached into the back to find what was making it stick.

His hand closed around a stack of envelopes tied together with a string. He pulled the package out and glanced at the address on the top one.

His name was written in a small, feminine hand, the postmark more than twenty years old.

He stared at the envelope for a long time, his emotions jerking him around like he was riding a bronc and couldn't get off.

His mother's handwriting on letters to him.

Cord's throat worked, but he couldn't swallow as he ripped open the first letter—a letter he'd never seen, never read. The envelope was postmarked in Austin, only a week after his mother had left the Flying Ace.

My dearest son, I miss you so much and I want you to understand— His vision blurred as he read word-for-word the letter his father had never given him. Had never mentioned. Cord swiped his eyes with the back of his hand as he ripped open the next letter, and the next.

His father had all the power, she'd said. She was trying to gain custody of Cord, but his father was blocking her, the attorneys battling each other. She wanted Cord to understand.

She loved him.

Letter after letter she wrote about the custody case, her longing to see Cord, to rock him to sleep at night as she had when he was little. She'd do it again now if she had the chance, even though he was practically full grown and would probably be embarrassed.

He'd wanted her to hold him; he remembered that. How tough it had been to act grown-up when all he'd wanted was to see his mom again. Be held like he was just a little kid.

Cord's vision blurred more than once as he read through the letters, and he had to wipe away the tears. His throat was raw with pain and grief.

By the time he reached the last of the letters, his emotions were tangled in his gut—joy that his mother had loved him, anger at his father for keeping the truth from him.

The final letter, postmarked a year after she'd left, wasn't from his mother, but from a stranger, a friend of his mother, she said. Inside the envelope she'd tucked a newspaper clipping. *His mother was dead.*

Cord sobbed aloud. His shoulders shook. A car accident. Highway 35. She'd been coming to see him to take him to a place they could be together.

As his tears dropped onto the yellowed newsprint, a weight lifted from his heart. Since his mother had abandoned him, he'd always thought he was unlovable. But that wasn't true. She'd been driven away by his father's infidelity and her own sense of morality.

The sound of Allie's soft voice echoed in his head.

Your mother thought of you constantly. More than anything else, she wanted you to be happy.

His mother had loved him.

Looking up, he glanced around the cluttered storage room at the mess. Allie had known, just looking at his baby pictures, that his mother had loved him. Her intuition had been more accurate than his own memories. His fears.

Maybe he could give Allie what she wanted, too.

His love.

But now he wasn't sure that would be enough.

Clearly, he needed a woman's advice before he made a total fool of himself. Again.

CORD CAUGHT BRIANNA ALONE early the next morning.

Acting casual, he poured himself a cup of coffee and leaned back against the kitchen counter. "I guess you got everything settled all right up in New Hampshire?"

She looked up from the bowl of cereal she was eating. "The papers are all signed, sealed and delivered."

"That's good. Very good." He felt as though someone had stuffed his mouth with cotton. This was his little sister, for God's sake. How could he ask her advice about women? About Allie?

She looked at him expectantly.

He cleared his throat and shoved away from the

counter. "Just wanted to make sure everything had gone okay."

"There isn't something else you'd like to ask me?"

"No, no. Just making sure." He started to leave the kitchen. Maybe he could ask Vi for advice. She ought to know what went on in a woman's head. Except he'd probably be so tongue-tied, he'd never get out a coherent sentence.

"Something about Allie?" Brianna asked.

Confounded, he wheeled around. "What do you mean?"

Lifting her mug of coffee, she took a sip, then smiled over the lip of the cup. "I thought maybe you wanted to find out how you can get Allie to marry you."

He went back to the table, sat down. Hope tangled in his throat. "You think she would?"

"If you don't make your proposal sound like you're the drill sergeant and she's the recruit, she might."

"I didn't do that. I made a reasonable suggestion that was in her own best interests, and she—"

"Turned you down flat."

Twice. Setting his cup down, he leaned his chin on his fist. "So what do I have to do?"

"First of all, do you love her?"

"You don't think it would be going off the deep end too fast if I do? She only came here a couple of weeks ago."

"Trust your heart, Cord. From what I saw, you were pretty well smitten that first day."

Swallowing his embarrassment, he nodded. "Yeah, I was, and I love her now."

Brianna's smile was so sweet, Cord was suddenly struck by what a beautiful young woman she was, and he wondered why no man had noticed yet. She had great hair, a really nice shade of blond, and beautiful, clear blue eyes. Of course, his preference at the moment was for pecan-brown hair and soul-deep eyes.

"It will be pretty important for you to tell her that. It's what a woman needs to hear."

"Okay, I can do that." It wouldn't be easy. A lot like sticking his neck in a noose and hoping a trapdoor didn't open up beneath his feet. But for Allie he'd take the risk.

"You'd also be wise to fulfill her fantasies, give her the proposal she's always dreamed about."

"I'm a Texas cowboy. I'm not really into fulfilling fantasies. I just want her to marry me." And have his babies. Grow old with him. Ordinary stuff like that.

Brianna studied her coffee a moment, then looked up again. "I may be giving away a confidence, but as a young girl Allie dreamed of some desert sheikh in flowing robes climbing over the wall into the women's quarters some dark night and whisking her off to his desert hideaway on his sleek Arabian steed."

"You're kidding."

"Nope."

"The only sheikh around here is her brother, and I don't think that's who she has in mind."

"Cord, are you being intentionally dense? Or are you just being a man?"

He glowered at his sister. "Okay, spell it out for me. What am I supposed to do?"

HE DIDN'T MANAGE TO GET Rafe alone until after dinner.

"Another game of backgammon or shall we try something else tonight?" Rafe asked as they walked into the living room.

Cord's mother had decorated the room when she'd first come here—with Western paintings, comfortable furniture, a bronze bucking bronco on the end table. In the past it had been difficult for Cord to look at the objects she had chosen and then rejected, along with rejecting him. But he'd been wrong on both counts.

Tonight he thought his mother would be pleased with his decision. *She'd wanted him to be happy.*

"Actually, I've got other plans for tonight."

Rafe glanced at him. "Oh. Well, do not trouble yourself about me. I will be fine on my own."

"I'm going over to the Desert Rose to propose to your sister."

Rafe didn't speak for a moment. "I believe Aliah has already turned you down once."

"I didn't go about it right the first time." Or the second. "Now I've got a better plan."

"If you are trying to be noble—make an honest woman of her, as they say—I can assure you that is not necessary. Whomever I pick as her husband will understand—"

"I don't want her to marry anyone else. I love her, and I believe she loves me."

Walking to the window, Rafe looked outside. Twilight was fading fast. "I find this situation… unsettling. In our country—"

"I'm not asking your permission, Rafe. I'm going to propose to Allie tonight. If she says yes—and I hope to God she does—we'll be married as soon as possible. I'm sure both she and I would like to have your blessing."

After a silent moment, Rafe turned and nodded. "You have it." He smiled slightly. "And if I know my sister, there may also be days when you will need my sympathy. I suspect she will not always be a pliable wife."

Cord laughed. "Maybe not, but she won't be boring, either."

The two men clasped hands, and Cord said, "There is one more thing I need from you, something I'd like to borrow."

"Whatever I have is yours."

Chapter Fourteen

At the Desert Rose, Allie stepped out of the shower, dried herself and slipped her nightgown on over her head.

Caring for twin babies was more difficult than she had imagined. To do that for two days in a row with two different sets of twins had taxed her energy. She had always assumed babies of the same age and same parentage would at least nap at the same time, giving the caregiver a few moments of peace and quiet. Obviously, her assumption had been incorrect.

But nothing in the world except having her own babies would have left her feeling more fulfilled by her two days of work—having her own babies with Cord, that is.

Sighing at her inability to get Cord out of her mind, she went into the bedroom. She picked up her brush and, standing before a full-length mirror, began to stroke her hair. Tomorrow she would stay a few hours with Abbie's eleven-month-old baby, Sarah. Perhaps caring for one child would be easier than two.

A light breeze shifted the curtains on the open

doors to the veranda, bringing with it the scent of freshly mowed grass and the roses growing up the trellis. She heard a noise outside but thought little of it. As she had learned at the Flying Ace, all sorts of wild creatures roamed a ranch at night. She need not concern herself with their activities.

She heard another noise. A loud thump.

Whirling, she opened her mouth to scream when she saw a white-robed man wearing a turban. He was half hanging over the veranda wall, snatching at his robe, which appeared to be snagged on the roses. Was she being kidnapped back to Munir?

The man grunted something that sounded much like an American curse. "Allie, it's me. Cord."

Her mouth remained open, but she didn't utter a word.

"Could you help me out here, Mischief? The ladder I brought wasn't long enough and this damn trellis isn't going to hold my weight much longer. I'm stuck."

The spell broken, she raced out onto the veranda. She grabbed his arm, tugging, astonished by Cord's appearance. "Have you gone mad? What are you doing here? Someone will hear you."

"This will be a lot easier to explain once I get up there. These roses are full of thorns. The robe's stuck—" Another grunt and the fabric ripped. Cord heaved himself over the top of the wall, half falling into Allie's arms. Torn between surprise and laughter, she helped steady him.

"I do not believe the Colemans lock their front

door at night. That might have been an easier way for you to drop by for a visit.''

''But not nearly as dramatic.''

She peered over the edge of the veranda. Below, a sleek Arabian horse stood munching on garden flowers, while patiently waiting for his rider's return. A little flutter of excitement rolled through Allie's midsection.

''What's this all about, Cord?''

''I think now I'm supposed to sweep you into my arms and carry you off to my tent at some desert oasis.'' He glanced over the side of the veranda to where a ladder leaned against the house a good six feet from the top of the wall. ''But my guess is if I tried that I'd get us both killed. So I'll have to ask you right here.''

''Ask me what?'' *Another proposal?* She couldn't go on doing this, turning him down because he didn't love her. Too soon she would weaken. Her heart would overrule what her head knew she needed—his love.

He took off the turban, tossing it aside. His hair was mussed, his eyes intense in the moonlight, and he took her hand in his. ''Princess Aliah Bahram, would you make me the happiest man in the world by doing me the honor of becoming my wife?''

''I have told you before I will not. Why should I change my mind now?'' *Please give me the answer I long to hear.*

''I love you, Allie. With all my heart.''

Hope blossomed more wildly than the roses of

summer. "How can I be sure you love me?" *In the name of Constantine, please let his love be true.*

"You mean beyond the fact I risked making a fool of myself by climbing up here and possibly breaking my neck in the process?"

"Yes, beyond that."

Raising her hand, he brushed a sweet kiss on her knuckles. "I worry that you weren't raised to live on a ranch, and that marrying me wouldn't be the smartest thing you could do. But even if it's wrong for you, I still can't get you out of my head, Mischief. I think about you all day long. I can't sleep at night. When I think about never seeing you again, never holding you again, I come close to going crazy with grief. Or maybe I'm already there."

She closed her eyes and let the sweet joy of happiness wash over her.

"If that's not love, Princess, I don't know what is."

"I believe we share a similar problem," she whispered, "for I think of you both day and night, every waking and sleeping moment. I dream of your kisses, the way it felt to be in your arms, and I long to be there again. I love you, Cord Brannigan. I always will."

"You know ranching can be a hard life."

"A life with you is what I yearn for."

"Then you'll marry me?" Relief trembled in his voice.

"Yes, master, in this one thing I am happy to do your bidding and marry you." She grinned at him, and standing on tiptoe, she brushed a kiss to his lips.

"Of course, after we are wed I will expect you to do as *I* ask."

His dark brows pulled together. "Just what did you have in mind?"

"That you make love with me every night so that we can make many babies together."

Laughing, he wrapped his arms around her and pulled her tight against his chest. "I'm pretty sure I can handle that. In fact, I'd like to get started right now." He glanced over the side again. "How 'bout instead of me whisking you off to some desert tent, we make love here in your bedroom?"

She widened her eyes in mock astonishment. "You do not think Mrs. Coleman—Vi—would find such an act scandalous?"

"I used to think Vi was exactly the kind of mother I wished I'd had. Right about now, I figure both Vi and my own mother would think I was the luckiest man in the world to have a woman like you loving me."

"In that we can all agree." This time Allie kissed him more deeply, her mouth lingering on his. "And I am by far the most fortunate woman on earth. I love you so much."

Without another word, he swept her up into his arms, carried her inside and proved to her beyond all doubt just how fortunate she was to have found her own true love in this once distant land called Texas.

THE WEDDING TOOK PLACE the following week at the Desert Rose. Cord had been too impatient to wait, and so had Allie, both more than willing to accept Vi's offer to host the ceremony in her home.

Even so, Allie had never been so nervous in her life. Her hands trembled as Leila helped her don the gold bracelets, earrings and necklace that had been her mother's and her mother's mother's for as many generations as memory could recall. Her unsteadiness caused the bracelets to make a shimmery sound as they moved together.

Leila stood back to inspect Allie's appearance. "You are a beautiful bride, my mistress."

"I'm glad you were able to be here. It is good to have someone at my wedding from home, even if you are missing your young man from the bazaar," Allie teased.

Making a show of indifference, Leila picked up the robe that would cover Allie's gown, in the Munir tradition, and shook it out. "He is not my young man."

"He's not? But I thought he smiled at you."

"It seems he smiles at all young women in that way, despite the fact he already has a wife."

"Oh, Leila, I'm sorry."

Her lady-in-waiting shrugged off her sympathy. "My only concern, now that you will not longer need my services, is where I shall live."

Allie hadn't considered that problem. She'd assumed Leila would continue to stay at the palace. But with Allie living in America, her lady-in-waiting would have few duties.

Suddenly an idea struck her. "Do you like babies?" Allie asked.

"Oh, yes, very much. I have dreamed that some-day—"

"If you could stay in America and work as a nanny, would you be willing?"

The enthusiasm that sparkled in Leila's dark eyes told Allie all she needed to know. The young Coleman wives still needed help with their babies and would for some years, since there would no doubt be more births in the family. Meanwhile, Allie assumed Cord would keep her so busy—and hopefully get her pregnant soon—that she would no longer be able to continue her baby-sitting job.

Leila would make a perfect replacement nanny.

"My mistress, the time has come for you to meet your groom."

The thrill of anticipation replaced Allie's anxiety as Leila helped her into the flowing robe and carefully pinned her veil in place, covering her face in the traditional way. With Leila following her, and her head held high, Allie walked out of her bedroom and down the curving staircase into the entryway, turning toward the spacious formal living room with its high ceiling—almost like a palace room.

Everyone was there—Vi and her husband, Randy; all of the Coleman sons and their wives, with their babies. Jessica and her husband, Nick, had driven in from Dallas yesterday. Even Rose Coleman-El Jeved Al Farid, for whom the ranch was named and who Allie had only just met, had returned to Texas for the ceremony with her husband, Zakariyya, the former king of Balahar and Rena's adoptive father.

And among the group were Cord's ranch hands, all dressed up in their finest clothes, with fancy Western shirts and string ties.

And, of course, Allie's brother and Cord's sister, both smiling in approval of the ceremony.

But the one person who drew Allie's gaze, as though she had traveled an endless desert in search of water and finally found what she had been seeking, was Cord.

Straight and tall, impossibly handsome in an ivory-colored, Western-cut suit, he stood beside the judge from Austin who would marry them.

Allie walked directly toward Cord, her heart so filled with happiness she thought surely it would burst. She stopped in front of him and smiled, although she knew he couldn't see her smile because of her veil.

"Ladies and gentlemen," the judge began.

"Hold it just a minute, Your Honor," Cord interrupted. "This is one time when I want to be darn sure I've got the right woman exactly where I want her."

Carefully, he released the veil that covered her face. When it fell away, he smiled, his eyes twinkling with mischief. "Yep, this is the one I had in mind to marry. You can go ahead now, Judge. And feel free to make it as quick as you can. I'm anxious to get on with the honeymoon."

Everyone in the room laughed, and so did Allie as the judge began to speak the words that would bind her to Cord for the rest of her life—and beyond.

CORD DIDN'T ONCE let go of Allie's hand after the ceremony was over. He felt like he was dreaming, that somehow she would slip away and he'd lose her.

With a glass of punch in his hand, Rafe stepped up to congratulate them. "The house of Bahram is honored to have you as a member of the family."

"Thanks, Rafe." Cord chuckled. "The Brannigans are okay with you being a member of the clan, too."

"Will you be going back to Munir now?" Allie asked her brother.

"Actually..." He set the empty punch cup aside. "Khalahari is very near her time. I thought I would remain in Bridle in the hope that I could see her foal."

"Sounds reasonable to me," Cord said. "Why don't you hang out at the Flying Ace? It'd be a lot more comfortable than staying in town."

"That's very kind of you, but—"

"Besides, you'd be able to keep an eye on Brianna while we're off on our honeymoon."

Brianna, who'd been standing nearby, turned around. "I really don't need anyone watching out for me, Cord. In fact—"

"Hey, it's a big house, little sister." Cord made an expansive gesture with his free hand. "The two of you probably won't see each other more than a couple of times a day. Rafe will be hanging out over here at the Desert Rose most of the time, anyway."

Cord wasn't sure what he'd done wrong. His sister was shooting daggers at him, and Allie was squeezing his hand so hard it hurt.

"Maybe we should go now, sweetheart," she said insistently.

Cord wasn't going to argue with her invitation. He'd planned a honeymoon that didn't include much sightseeing beyond the four walls of an elegant hotel room. With luck, he'd make Allie's wish come true.

She'd be pregnant by the time they returned to the Flying Ace. *This* time he'd been dealt a perfect hand—the ace of hearts was high.

* * * * *

Don't miss
BY THE SHEIKH'S COMMAND
by Debbi Rawlins,
the final installment of the
BRIDES OF THE DESERT ROSE
series, on sale for
Harlequin American Romance
in August 2002.

Princes...Princesses...
London Castles...New York Mansions...
To live the life of a royal!

In 2002, Harlequin Books lets you escape to a world of royalty with these royally themed titles:

Celebrate a year of royalty with Harlequin Books!

Available at your favorite retail outlet.

HARLEQUIN®
Makes any time special®
Visit us at www.eHarlequin.com

HSROY02

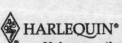

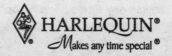